THE LOST SWORD

BLOOMSBURY

LONDON OXFORD NEW DELHI NEW YORK SYDNEY

Bloomsbury Publishing, London, Oxford, New York, New Delhi and Sydney

First published in Great Britain in July 2015 by Bloomsbury Publishing Plc
50 Bedford Square, London WC1B 3DP

www.bloomsbury.com

Bloomsbury is a registered trademark of Bloomsbury Publishing Plc

A CIP catalogue record for this book is available from the British Library

ISBN 978 1 4088 4758 9

Typeset by Integra Software Services Pvt. Ltd.
Printed and bound in Great Britain by CPI Group (UK) Ltd, Croydon CR0 4YY

1 3 5 7 9 10 8 6 4 2

THE LOST SWORD

For my son, Carter

Prologue

Deep Space

'There's a storm brewing.'

Baden Scott stood on the bridge of his salvage trawler, the *Rough Diamond III*, clutching a flask of coffee and staring through the window at the distant stars. His crew had been cruising deep space for almost a week in search of scrap, but the only thing they had recovered beyond the seven solar systems was a stray satellite. If they didn't find something valuable soon, Baden would be forced to sell his holiday home on Reus.

'You're right, the scanners are picking up activity in the asteroid field ahead,' said Kiki, the pilot. 'I'll give it a wide berth.'

Baden smiled and rubbed his stubbly chin. 'I love a good space storm. Nothing can stop those big old rocks once they start moving. If anything gets in their way, they crush it and sweep it aside, no questions asked.'

'That sounds like the Interstellar Navy,' said Kiki, pulling on the controls.

'You're not wrong.' Baden laughed and swigged his coffee. 'Mind you, I would rather take my chances with those asteroids. At least they play fair.'

The *Rough Diamond III* changed course and headed further into deep space, where few ships dared to go. There wasn't much to salvage that far out, but at least no one would try to spacejack their new trawler.

'Hey, Baden.'

'Yes?'

'I'm picking up something on the long-range scanner.' Kiki adjusted her display. 'There's a cluster of shapes heading towards the seventh solar system.'

'More asteroids?'

'I don't think so; they're in battle formation.'

'Battle formation?' choked out Baden. 'Are you sure?'

'Yeah, like a fleet of warships, but what would the Interstellar Navy be doing out here?'

'There's only one reason why that many ships would be sneaking through deep space.' Baden drained his coffee and popped a wad of chewing gum into his mouth. 'War.'

Kiki looked horrified. 'What war? You mean those ships are going to attack an independent colony?'

'Why stop at one?' said Baden, chewing grimly. 'There's enough laser power in that fleet to take out the entire seventh solar system. I suggest we get out of here before we're spotted.'

'Where do you want to go?'

'Set course for the sixth solar system.' Baden watched the shapes on the long-range scanner. 'We can find work there, while the storm blows over.'

Chapter 1

The Trading Station

The *ISS Timidus* loomed over the trading station like a hunched metal spectre. It was one of nine naval gunships patrolling the fifth solar system, with orders to protect the crystal trade routes from space pirates. Gunships were smaller than warships and they carried less crew, but they were faster and able to bear heavy laser cannon.

In comparison, the trading station resembled a large copper doughnut suspended in space. Its tarnished hull contained rows of porthole windows, which glowed with warm amber light. The traders were used to raids, only this time the *ISS Timidus* wasn't searching for stolen ship parts or illegal weapons, but something far more dangerous.

Inside, naval troops in midnight blue uniforms herded traders and customers to the central atrium, where they gathered below a spiral escalator. A senior officer paced the floor, his polished gravity boots clipping the metal grating. He surveyed the crowd with narrow bloodshot eyes, but most of their faces were concealed under traditional wide-brimmed hats.

'What's the point of these ridiculous things in space?' he asked, snatching one from a female trader and throwing it across the atrium. 'I'm going to ask you wretchards one more time: have any of you seen a cargo hauler named the *Dark Horse?*'

No one spoke.

'Admiral Vantard has reason to believe that this pirate ship was responsible for the disappearance of the *ISS Colossus* super-destroyer three months ago,' said the officer. 'He's particularly keen to talk with the crew and their teenage captain, Jake Cutler –'

One of the male traders snorted, causing the officer to turn sharply.

'Is there something funny about a child spacejacker?'

The trader was a large man with pale skin and huge arms. He raised his head and stared back with wolf-like eyes.

'Well?' demanded the officer.

'My friend doesn't speak much,' said a bronze-skinned man next to him. 'But I'm sure he didn't mean any offence.'

The officer glared at the pair of them, like an impatient teacher with two disruptive pupils.

'There's a reward for the boy,' he said, stepping back to address the wider crowd. 'A crate of crystals for his capture. He can be identified by his brown hair, purple eyes and gold pendant –'

'What about his cutlass?' interrupted a younger trader.

'What about it?' snapped the officer, rounding on the boy and swiping the hat from his head.

'It's very sharp,' said the trader, producing a cutlass from inside his coat.

The officer took one look at the boy's bright purple eyes and raised his arms.

'Jake Cutler?'

'Captain Cutler, according to you.' Jake prodded the officer in the stomach. 'Tell your troops to drop their weapons before I gut you with my blade.'

Jake was no ordinary teenager. He was a space pirate and the ruler of a secret planet, Altus. It hadn't always been this way. Until a few months ago, Jake had lived with cyber-monks on Remota, a secluded planet in the seventh solar system. He had grown up not knowing who he was or where he was from. His only clue had been a gold pendant containing three crystals: a diamond, a ruby and an emerald.

When the monastery was attacked by naval troops disguised as space pirates, Jake had escaped

Remota aboard an old cargo hauler called the *Dark Horse*, which turned out to be a pirate ship belonging to the Space Dogs. With their help, Jake had discovered Altus hiding inside the Tego Nebula dust cloud. But not before they had defeated Admiral Nex and his super-destroyer, the *ISS Colossus*.

'Now hold on ...' said the officer.

The naval troops saw what was happening and turned their plasma rifles on Jake, who responded by nudging his sword a little harder. He had never gutted anyone in his life, but the troops didn't know that. As far as they were concerned, he had single-handedly destroyed the *ISS Colossus*, making him more dangerous than other famous pirates, such as James Hawker or Scarabus Shark. Jake had earned himself the nickname Kid Cutler.

'You heard him,' said the officer, his voice now several pitches higher. 'Drop your weapons, that's an order.'

The troops lowered their plasma rifles and placed them on the floor. Three space pirates shed their disguises and stepped from the crowd to collect the guns, including the large pale man, Kodan, his bronze-skinned friend, Farid, and a muscular shipmate with thick dreadlocks, Woorak. The crowd dispersed around them, as traders and customers abandoned the station before more troops arrived.

'*Captain* Cutler?' said Farid, who was the first mate aboard the *Dark Horse*.

'Why not?' laughed Jake. 'You have to admit, there's a certain ring to it.'

Farid raised an eyebrow. 'Wait until the real captain finds out that you're after her job.'

'It's OK,' said Jake. 'I'm not in a hurry to lead anyone.'

After removing his uncle Kear from power, Jake had taken his rightful place as the ruler of Altus, only to discover that he wasn't ready to lead. His home planet had not felt complete without his missing father, Andras Cutler. When the Space Dogs were forced to leave in a hurry, Jake had decided to go with them and continue his search for his father. It had not been easy to abandon his people, but how else would he find the true ruler of Altus?

'What do you want with us, spacejacker?' asked the naval officer.

'With you? Nothing,' said Jake. 'We just need to borrow your gunship for a while.'

Kodan grinned. He was the master-at-arms, responsible for keeping peace aboard the *Dark Horse*, despite being unable to speak a word.

Farid produced a communicator from his pocket. 'Ahoy, Callidus. We've secured our guests. How are you and Capio getting on?'

Callidus Stone was an ex-naval officer turned fortune seeker. He had spent years searching for Altus with his clumsy companion, Capio Craven. Callidus had helped Jake to escape from Remota and find his home planet.

'Ahoy, Farid,' said Callidus. 'The crew didn't put up much of a fight. We're on the bridge now and I'm accessing their ship's computer. It shouldn't take long; not much has changed since I was in the Interstellar Navy.'

'You're aboard our ship?' exclaimed the officer.

'Yep,' said Jake. 'We need to access the main naval server to find out what you lot know about us, so we can keep one step ahead of you. And I want information about a ship that was destroyed eleven years ago.'

The communicator crackled.

'Hmm, that's interesting,' muttered Callidus.

'What is?' asked Farid.

'An old navy buddy of mine has retired.'

'Fascinating,' said Farid impatiently. 'Now hurry up and find something useful.'

'Why don't we take their ship?' asked Jake. 'Isn't that what spacejackers are supposed to do?'

'Yeah, right,' said Farid. 'I can just imagine turning up at the next service port in a naval gunship. It's not exactly discreet, is it?'

'W-w-we don't need another ship,' stuttered Woorak. 'Not now we have n-n-new registration plates and a coat of p-p-paint.'

'Ah,' said Callidus.

'What's up?' asked Farid.

'This isn't the only naval vessel in the area. A warship is approaching and it's hailing the gunship.'

'Ah,' echoed Farid.

A cold panic spread through Jake's body. It was bad enough to encounter a naval warship in open space, where they could at least make a run for it, but they were docked inside a trading station with the gunship crew as hostages.

'Get everyone back to the ship,' instructed Callidus. 'I'll delay them.'

'Let's go,' said Farid, backing towards the exit.

'Leaving so soon?' sneered the officer.

Jake flicked his cutlass with lightning speed and sliced open the officer's jacket. He watched the silver buttons spill on to the metal grating.

'Oops, sorry about that,' he said.

Farid, Kodan, Woorak and Jake hurried through a red arched walkway to the maintenance bay, where the rest of the crew were waiting. It was hard to run in gravity shoes and the air was thick with incense cubes, which were used to disguise the stench of recycled oxygen. As they reached the bay entrance, three people stumbled out of another passage holding midnight blue containers.

'Watch out,' warned Farid.

Kodan and Woorak instinctively raised the plasma rifles they had collected.

'Wait, don't shoot,' said a voice from behind one of the crates.

'Maaka?' recognised Jake.

'Aye,' said the shipmate, lowering his container. 'The captain sent us to get some supplies from the gunship.'

Maaka 'Metal Head' was a gnarly-looking ship-mate with a face full of scars and piercings. Next to him stood Jake's two teenage friends, Kella and Nanoo, their arms laden with naval supplies.

Kella Anderson was a United Worlds citizen and a talented crystal healer. Jake had often wondered how someone could cure people with shiny stones, but whenever he asked her, Kella just shrugged her shoulders and told him that it was a gift. Apparently, the crystals were only tools that helped to channel her healing powers, in the same way that a megaphone was used to amplify sound.

Jake had first met Kella in Papa Don's illegal spaceport, where she had been held for ransom because her family owned a crystal mine in the sixth solar system. Her sister, Jeyne, had been on her way to pay the ransom when the Interstellar Navy had arrested her, leaving Kella at the mercy of the space mafia. Jake had helped to free Kella, who was now part of the Space Dogs crew and the ship's medic.

Nanoo was a lilac-skinned Novu alien from planet Taan-Centaur in a distant galaxy. His exploration ship had crashed into an asteroid, killing his parents and the crew. He had been left alone, stranded for a whole year inside the shipwreck, before Jake discovered him.

What Nanoo lacked in language skills, he made up for with his knowledge of advanced alien technology, which he had used to make a number of improvements to the *Dark Horse*. This included engine enhancements, stronger electronic shields and more powerful laser cannon. All of which made the old cargo hauler much tougher than it looked.

Kella flicked aside her long black hair and opened a container full of food pouches. 'These naval munchies look much nicer than that stuff in the trader canteen.'

'And we disable gunship engine,' said Nanoo, his wide turquoise eyes sparkling with delight. 'They not go anywhere fast.'

'Good work,' approved Farid. 'But we need to hurry.'

In the maintenance bay, they were met by the chief engineer, Scargus, and his assistant, Manik.

'We can't leave yet,' protested Scargus. 'The ship is not ready.'

'Sorry, we don't have any choice,' said Farid. 'There's a naval warship heading our way.'

'But we've not tested the new boosters, the rear shields need calibrating and the intercom is faulty.'

'And the paint is still wet,' added Manik, holding up her artificial arm, which was covered in red flecks.

'Will she fly?' asked Farid.

'Aye,' said Scargus. 'But ...'

'That's all I need to know.' Farid headed straight for a cargo hauler with a plump red hull. 'Let's get the old girl into the stars.'

'I heard that,' croaked a silver-haired woman, standing at the top of the loading ramp. 'And you had better be talking about the ship.'

'Aye, captain.'

Granny Leatherhead was captain of the *Dark Horse*, which had served the Space Dogs for over twenty years. It had endured many adventures and its battle scars were still visible beneath the coat of paint. Jake had grown fond of the old cargo hauler. It was like one of the crew, a comrade in arms. Thanks to Nanoo, the ship now boasted four new booster exhausts and a multi-barrelled laser cannon hidden inside its nose.

'Isn't she a beauty,' sighed Scargus.

'Aye, she'll do,' said Farid, climbing the loading ramp.

'Now I know you're talking about me,' cackled Granny Leatherhead.

The captain was dressed in a faded black combat suit, which was covered in patches, straps and buckles. It was traditional for pirate crews to have their own colours and customise their outfits. A crusty leather patch covered one of her eyes, while the other looked down her hooked nose at the naval supplies.

'I hope you picked up something a bit stronger than fruit juice this time,' she said.

The maintenance bay doors crashed open and Callidus entered, closely followed by Capio. Jake noticed that the tall fortune seeker was holding a data crystal.

'Start the engine,' shouted Callidus, his long coat flapping behind him.

'What happened?' asked Farid, from the top of the loading ramp.

'It's the naval warship,' said Callidus. 'I didn't know the latest security codes.'

'How long before they're in range?' asked Granny Leatherhead.

'Two minutes.'

'Blast it.' The captain turned to a blue-haired woman waiting in the cargo hold. 'Nichelle, fire up the engine, we're leaving in one minute.'

'That's not all,' said Callidus, as he reached the bottom of the ramp. 'It's the *ISS Magnificent*. Admiral Vantard has tracked us down.'

Chapter 2

The Divine Wind

Jake and the Space Dogs had been blamed for the disappearance of Admiral Algor Nex, after he was sucked into a black hole along with his super-destroyer, the *ISS Colossus*. It was now common knowledge that Admiral Nex had been searching for a teenage space pirate with purple eyes. The name Jake Cutler had spread throughout the galaxy, as the boy who had defeated the most advanced warship in the Interstellar Navy.

Now there was a new admiral in charge, Voratio Vantard, the most decorated officer in naval history. His handsome face and dashing smile often featured on the stellar-net, with reports of daring feats and dangerous missions. His fine copper hair and bottle green uniform were smart even for a naval officer, prompting his nickname: Admiral Vaintard. If anyone wanted to be credited with capturing the most dreaded space pirate of all time, it was him.

The Space Dogs had been hunted by Admiral Vantard since leaving Altus, occasionally crossing laser cannon with his warship, the *ISS Magnificent*. If Nanoo hadn't used his alien technology to strengthen the cargo hauler's shields, the entire crew would have been stardust by now. But they could not survive on luck forever. It was only a matter of time before Admiral Vantard captured the *Dark Horse* and punished them for making the Interstellar Navy appear weak.

What if they were tortured and one of the crew revealed the secret location of Altus? Jake was starting to wonder if he had made the right decision to leave his home planet. He had put his people in danger to search for his missing father and he didn't know where to start. If only he knew what Andras Cutler looked like, or why he had stayed away for so long. Jake had not considered what would happen once they found his father. What if he didn't want anything to do with Altus? More to the point, what if he didn't want anything to do with Jake?

In the trading station, the *Dark Horse* rattled and clanked as the crew prepared for take-off. Jake hurried to the guest quarters, where he shared a room with Callidus and Capio. He climbed into his bunk and listened to the sound of the loading ramp close beneath the ship. It wasn't the first time they had launched in a hurry, but he still experienced a rush of adrenalin as the engine roared to life.

'Get yourselves strapped in quick, folks,' instructed Granny Leatherhead over the faulty intercom, her voice sounding deep and stretched. 'We're leaving as soon as the bay doors open.'

Jake fastened his buckles and lay flat on his bunk, staring at the flashing amber light on the ceiling. It had been good to stop running for a few days, but now it was time to flee the trading station. He wondered how much longer they could keep this up. Weeks? Months? Scargus had once told him that life as a space pirate was mostly hard work and hiding from the Interstellar Navy. It certainly seemed that way.

Nichelle released the thrusters, which thundered like an explosion refusing to end. Jake felt the *Dark Horse* surge towards the bay doors. His bunk vibrated as the ship gathered speed, bumping him against the bed straps. The bay walls blurred past the porthole window, until suddenly, without warning, they were replaced by stars as the old cargo hauler hurled itself into space.

'Hello, big black,' whispered Jake, releasing his straps and floating free from his bunk, no longer held down by artificial gravity.

He kicked off the nearest wall and propelled himself towards the window, so he could see what was happening outside. Through the scratched glass, he caught sight of the naval warship, its long midnight blue hull cutting through the stars. The name *ISS Magnificent* was printed on the side in tall white letters, each one larger than the *Dark Horse*.

Jake pushed himself away from the window and back to his bunk, where his home-made gravity shoes were stuck to the wall. He plucked them off the metal surface and slipped them on to his feet, allowing the magnetic soles to drag him to the floor.

'Where are you going?' asked Callidus.

'To the bridge,' said Jake. 'The captain might need our help.'

He climbed through the hatch door and hurried down the corridor, past the engine room, up the metal staircase and along the top deck to the front of the cargo hauler. As usual, Nichelle was piloting the ship, while Farid watched the scanners and Kodan stood silently by the door. Granny Leatherhead looked tired as she paced the floor.

'Captain, we're being hailed by the *ISS Magnificent*,' said Farid.

'Ignore them,' croaked Granny Leatherhead. 'They'll find out who we are soon enough, once they've spoken with the gunship crew. Nichelle, it's time to try out the new boosters.'

'Aye, captain.'

The pilot tightened her dark blue ponytail and punched several buttons on her control panel. Jake grabbed hold of the hatch and braced himself for acceleration.

'Wait,' said Farid. 'There's another ship in the way.'

'Who is it?' asked Granny Leatherhead, her single grey eye squinting at the main display.

'It's an old space cutter called the *Loose Cannon*, registered to a fortune seeker named Carla Gritt.'

'Not another meddling mercenary,' groaned Granny Leatherhead. 'That's the fifth one since leaving Altus. If the reward for our capture goes up much higher, I'll be tempted to hand myself in. Is her ship armed?'

'Aye, but it only has a single laser cannon,' said Farid. 'I'm more worried about the *ISS Magnificent* behind us, if our rear shields have not been calibrated.'

'So let's turnabout and face them.'

'But then our exhausts will be exposed to the *Loose Cannon*.'

Callidus and Capio entered the bridge.

'What's going on?' asked the fortune seeker. 'Why have we stopped?'

'Carla Gritt.' Granny Leatherhead pointed a wrinkled finger at the main display. 'Is she a friend of yours?'

'Gritt?' Callidus swept back his dark wavy hair, revealing two metal studs fixed to the sides of his head. 'I've only ever heard of her by reputation. Carla Gritt would sell her own parents for a fist full of crystals.'

'Captain, the *ISS Magnificent* is still hailing us,' said Farid. 'I don't think the new registration plates have worked. They're preparing their laser cannon.'

'Blast it,' cursed Granny Leatherhead, holding her forehead. 'Nichelle, get us out of here.'

'I can't,' said the pilot. 'The *Loose Cannon* is matching our every move.'

'Then ram her out of the way.'

'No,' said Jake, watching from the doorway. 'We'll rupture our hull.'

'Who asked you?'

'He's right,' said Callidus. 'A collision is too risky, even with our strengthened shields.'

'OK, fine,' snapped the captain. 'Blow her to stardust.'

'If we do that, the naval warship will open fire for sure,' said Farid.

'So what in the name of Zerost can we do?' Granny Leatherhead scowled at Callidus. 'This is all your fault.'

'Me?'

'Aye, you and your idiotic ideas. I can't believe you talked me into spacejacking a naval gunship. Was it worth it? Did its computer tell you anything useful?'

'No, but –'

'I knew it,' she barked. 'I must have been mad to let you lot join my crew.'

'Captain,' urged Farid. 'Both ships are preparing to fire.'

'We should surrender,' said Capio. 'Before it's too late.'

'Hah!' shrieked Granny Leatherhead. 'How long have you been on this ship? It's not in a Space Dog's nature to give up without a fight. Nichelle, turn the ship about to face the *ISS Magnificent*. We're going to blow a hole in its horrible hull, before Ms Gritt tears open our rear.'

'Aye, captain.'

'Are you insane?' said Callidus. 'That's suicide. I know we defeated the *ISS Colossus*, but it was already damaged and we were helped by a black hole. Capio's right, we have to surrender.'

'Stand down, Callidunce,' warned Granny Leatherhead. 'I'm the captain of this ship and I say we fight.'

'Surrender,' insisted the fortune seeker, reaching for his pistol.

'Fight,' she yelled, fetching her own gun.

The two of them stood inches apart, weapons drawn and eyes fixed on each other.

'Stop it,' shouted Jake. 'Don't we have enough enemies?'

'Captain,' interrupted Farid. 'There's a third ship.'

'Fine by me,' she said, not taking her eye off Callidus. 'Let's see how many it takes to bring down the Space Dogs.'

'It's a pirate ship.' Farid tapped feverishly on his display. 'A star frigate called the *Divine Wind*. It's heading straight for the *ISS Magnificent*.'

Granny Leatherhead almost dropped her pistol as she turned to look at the display screen. Jake caught sight of a bright yellow ship with a space pirate emblem painted on its hull, only the crew had used crossed feathers instead of bones. There was also a blood-red letter 'K' painted on the side and several pink laser cannon jutting out of its gun ports.

'It can't be the *Divine Wind*,' muttered Granny Leatherhead, her face whitening. 'Not after all these years.'

The yellow star frigate opened fire, catching the *ISS Magnificent* by surprise and scorching its hull, before it veered sharply and accelerated in the opposite direction. Jake could make out the words 'kiss my cutlass' written on its rear. He watched the naval warship change course to pursue the pirate ship, its own laser cannon blazing.

Granny Leatherhead turned her back on the screen. 'Now's our chance. Nichelle, head straight for Carla Gritt. Kodan, prepare Nanoo's latest invention in case she refuses to budge. It's time we left the fifth solar system.'

'Aye, captain,' said Nichelle, tugging at her controls.

Kodan nodded and marched over to a small panel beneath the main display, which he slid aside to reveal a secret compartment in the nose of the ship. Jake had watched Nanoo working on the multi-barrelled laser cannon, which they had nicknamed Old Lizzy after the captain. He knew that the crew were itching to try it out, especially Kodan, who now squeezed into the tight space.

Granny Leatherhead glared at the space cutter. 'Your move, nasty nickers.'

The *Dark Horse* drew closer, gathering speed, but the *Loose Cannon* held its position.

Jake spotted a hatch opening on its hull. 'Captain, she's up to something.'

A hose slithered out of the hole with a sprinkler attached to the end.

'That's no laser cannon,' said Farid.

'What is it?' asked Jake.

'That, my lad, is trouble,' said Granny Leatherhead. 'Brace yourself for an acid shower.'

'But they're illegal,' exclaimed Capio.

'So is spacejacking,' pointed out Callidus. 'Will the shields hold?'

'Let's not find out,' said Granny Leatherhead. 'Avast, Nichelle, pull back.'

'It's too late,' cried the blue-haired pilot.

Jake was shocked to see globules of green liquid spray from the sprinkler head, creating a web of acid in front of them. The *Dark Horse* ploughed straight through the toxic rain, which splattered across the front of the ship, burning holes in their shields and scarring the hull. At the same time, Carla Gritt opened fire with her single laser cannon.

'My lovely paint job,' screeched Granny Leatherhead. 'What are you waiting for, Kodan? Kill that sneaky space witch.'

Kodan pulled the trigger and a string of laser bolts fired in rapid succession, like splintered lightning exploding from the nose of the ship. His huge arms shook violently as he tried to control the multi-barrelled weapon. If Jake had thought the sawn-off laser cannon were loud, they were nothing compared to this booming beast. It used up so much power, the bridge lights dimmed and the computer displays flickered.

'Missed,' reported Farid.

Kodan grunted, took aim and fired again, this time scattering laser bolts like flaming buckshot. Jake watched as several of them exploded on Carla Gritt's shields.

'That's it,' said Granny Leatherhead. 'Keep shooting.'

The fortune seeker knew that she was outgunned and she changed her tactics. Her ship circled around the *Dark Horse*, targeting its exposed rear. Jake felt the hull shake as the cargo hauler received yet another battle scar.

'Maaka, Woorak, roll out the stubbies,' ordered Granny Leatherhead through the intercom, which now made her voice sound high-pitched and squeaky. 'Nichelle, turn us about, don't let her get a clean shot at our exhausts.'

Nichelle turned the *Dark Horse*, while hidden gun ports scraped open on the side of the hull to reveal a row of sawn-off laser cannon.

'Now, boys,' croaked Granny Leatherhead. 'Fire!'

Maaka and Woorak unleashed their cannon, spitting out laser bolts and forcing Carla Gritt to abandon her attack. As her ship peeled away, Nichelle swung the nose of the *Dark Horse* around and Kodan pumped out a third stream of laser bolts, penetrating the space cutter's shields and rupturing its hull.

'Direct hit,' cheered Farid. 'Her systems are down, finish her off.'

'Don't waste the lasers,' said Granny Leatherhead. 'Let space have her.'

Kodan ceased fire, leaving a ringing silence in the air. Jake watched the *Loose Cannon* on the computer display, damaged and adrift. He felt a sudden pity for the fortune seeker. What if that had been Callidus?

But Granny Leatherhead showed no remorse. 'Nichelle, get us out of here before that naval warship returns.'

'Aye, captain.'

Nichelle accelerated away from the trading station, putting as many stars as possible between the *Dark Horse* and the *ISS Magnificent*.

'Captain.'

'Yes, Jake?'

'Who owns the *Divine Wind*?'

Chapter 3

Wild Joe Jagger

It had been three hours since the *Dark Horse* had left the trading station. A rumour was spreading through the ship that they had run out of places to hide, which was fuelled further when Granny Leatherhead summoned the crew to the dining area on the first deck. Jake strapped himself into a seat next to Kella and Nanoo. The captain stood on a table, clutching a star chart in one hand and rubbing her forehead with the other.

'OK, folks, let's start with the good news,' she said. 'There's no sign of the *ISS Magnificent* on the long-range scanner. It looks as though we've made a clean getaway.'

There was a ripple of half-hearted cheers from the crew. Jake knew that everyone was thinking the same thing.

'We would have been scuppered back there,' said Farid. 'If it hadn't been for the *Divine Wind*.'

'Yeah, who were those spacejackers?' asked Maaka.

'I've already told you,' croaked Granny Leatherhead. 'I don't know.'

'But you recognised the ship,' said Callidus.

Granny Leatherhead stiffened. 'I've not seen the *Divine Wind* for over a decade. As far as I knew, that old star frigate was sold for scrap when its captain died. Has anyone heard of Wild Joe Jagger?'

Most of the crew shook their heads.

'I have,' said Scargus. 'His crew used to take on the most dangerous jobs that no one else would touch. He was responsible for the Ranko prison break and the Cortis gold heist.'

'Aye, that's him,' said Granny Leatherhead. 'Wild Joe earned his reputation as one of the most daring and reckless spacejackers in the seven solar systems.'

'How did he die?' asked Jake.

'Not well,' said Scargus. 'His body was found strapped to the hull of his ship. The crew were floating nearby, having been made to walk the airlock without spacesuits.'

'Interstellar Navy do it?' asked Nanoo.

'Unlikely,' said Granny Leatherhead. 'If they had caught a space pirate, they would have wanted the whole galaxy to know about it. No, I reckon he was killed by someone he knew. Wild Joe was quite a character, but not everyone liked his style. He had his share of enemies, the same as the rest of us.'

'What are you saying?' asked Callidus. 'We were rescued by a ghost?'

'Don't be ridiculous,' she snapped. 'The *Divine Wind* must have a new crew. At least they were prepared to fight. If it had been up to you, we would all be prisoners by now.'

'If it had been up to you, we would all be dead by now.'

'Please don't start that again,' said Jake.

Farid pointed to the star chart in her hand. 'Where are we heading, captain?'

Granny Leatherhead looked down, as though she had forgotten what she was holding. 'Ah, yes, that's the bad news. We need to find somewhere for Scargus and Manik to finish repairing the ship. It would also be nice to stay in the same place for a while.'

'What about my dad?' asked Jake.

'What about him? We can't keep stumbling around the galaxy hoping to bump into your father. The crew needs some proper rest. You can use the time to come up with a plan to find him. He's been missing for eleven years, so a few more weeks or months won't harm.'

'Where did you have in mind?' asked Nichelle.

'That's the problem. I've trawled the charts, but there aren't any safe ports nearby and we've used up all of our best hideouts. Does anyone have any ideas?'

It appeared that the rumour was true and they had run out of places to hide.

'Papa Don's illegal spaceport?' suggested Maaka.

'Too far,' said Granny Leatherhead. 'Besides, I don't think the space mafia would be pleased to see us right now. Not while we're the most wanted crew in the galaxy.'

'How about the t-t-trading station?' stammered Woorak. 'Admiral Vantard w-w-won't expect us to d-d-double back.'

'Nice idea, but for all we know the *ISS Magnificent* might still be there.'

'How about you, Callidus?' asked Farid. 'What did you learn from the naval gunship?'

'I found out that Admiral Vantard has warships searching for us in every solar system. There were also files about fleet deployments and Gorks, but I was unable to access them.'

'Fleet deployments?' said Nichelle. 'That doesn't sound good.'

'Who is Gorks?' asked Nanoo.

'Aliens,' said Jake. 'Gorks are the last known "intelligent" species to be discovered, but they're not what I would call intelligent.'

'They first made contact about fifty years ago,' explained Callidus. 'Their planet had become unstable, forcing them to leave their galaxy on space rafts to seek out a new home. Gorks are large and strong, with rubbery blue skin and fins on their heads, but they are also simple and clumsy. The United Worlds use them as cheap labour in factories and shipyards. Not many people like Gorks living on their planets, because they tend to be violent and messy.'

Granny Leatherhead cleared her throat with such force, it sounded like a hover-bike taking off.

'As much as I enjoy gabbing about those gormless guffoons, it's not going to help us to fix this ship or find a place to stay. There must be somewhere we can go?'

Her eye darted expectantly around the room.

'Not even the independent colonies are safe these days,' said Manik.

'And we would stick out like kalmar poo on a fancy United Worlds planet,' commented Scargus.

'You most welcome on Taan-Centaur,' said Nanoo. 'We could build Novu engine and take *Dark Horse* to my galaxy, where no one find us.'

Capio looked horrified. 'No offence, Nanoo, but even if we could afford the parts, I'm not sure that I would want to live that far away.'

'Agreed,' croaked Granny Leatherhead. 'There must be somewhere suitable in this galaxy.'

'We need inside knowledge,' said Callidus. 'My old navy buddy, Helen Brack, has just retired in this solar system. I expect that she still has some useful contacts and she might know of a safe planet.'

'Why in the name of Zerost would she help us?' asked Granny Leatherhead.

'Helen owes me,' said Callidus. 'I saved her life a few times.'

Farid shook his head. 'Space pirates don't trust anyone, especially not ex-naval officers.'

'You trust me, don't you?' said Callidus, impatiently. 'I was a captain in the Interstellar Navy.'

'It's still not safe for you to contact your friend from this ship,' insisted the first mate. 'What if she decides to report our location?'

'It's not as though we can go and see her in person.'

'Now there's a good idea,' said Granny Leatherhead with a malicious smile. 'I reckon you should go and visit your friend. At least that would get your miserable mug off my cargo hauler for a few days.'

Callidus tensed and his eyes narrowed. 'Is that right?'

'Aye, we can drop you and Capio at the next spaceport, where you can catch a ride on a passenger ship. You can come back when you have some useful information.'

Callidus looked furious. After everything they had been through, the captain was kicking him and Capio off the ship.

'Fine,' he said, through clenched teeth. 'Capio and I could do with a break from these rusty walls. But what about the rest of you? Where will you go?'

Scargus stood up. 'He's got a point; the *Dark Horse* is still in urgent need of repair. We have to find somewhere to stop for a couple of days.'

'I've got an idea,' said Jake.

'We're not going back to Altus, Kid Cutler,' grumped Granny Leatherhead.

'I know, that's not what I was going to suggest. There's a monastery on planet Shan-Ti in the fourth solar system. I was supposed to go there when I left Remota. The cyber-monks might let us dock for a few days.'

'A monastery, eh?' mused Granny Leatherhead.

'Yes, I can tell them that Father Pius sent me.'

'We're not far from the fourth solar system,' said Farid. 'It's worth a try.'

'OK, why not.' Granny Leatherhead turned to Nichelle. 'Once we've dropped Callidus and Capio, set course for Shan-Ti. I want you to stay alert and ready for trouble. The first hint of Admiral Vantard and we're out of there.'

The captain stepped down from the table and left the room. Jake noticed that she was limping slightly. The rest of the crew finished their drinks and returned to their posts.

'That sorted,' said Nanoo, stretching. 'You know cyber-monks well?'

'No, I've never met them.'

'How do you know they'll help us?' asked Kella.

'I don't,' said Jake. 'But it's the best idea we've got. If we're lucky, they might let me use their computers to search for more clues about my dad.'

Callidus approached their table. 'Jake, can I have a word?'

'Yes, of course.'

The fortune seeker cast a sideways glance at Kella and Nanoo. 'In private.'

'Oh, right.' Jake turned to the others. 'I'll catch you up.'

Kella and Nanoo followed Capio out of the dining area and down the metal staircase. Callidus waited until their footsteps had faded away. It was the first time that Jake had been alone with him since the trading station. Callidus no longer seemed like the confident fortune seeker that Jake had first met. He had been moody since leaving Altus and now spent his time lazing in bed or moping about the ship. His nails were chipped and his thick black stubble had turned into a beard. But despite this, Jake was going to miss him.

'Do you really have to go, Cal?'

'It looks that way.'

'I wish that I could come with you.'

'No, it's too dangerous. What if you were recognised? Trust me, you'll be safer on Shan-Ti.'

Jake somehow doubted it. The last monastery to offer him sanctuary had been burnt to the ground. But he knew that Granny Leatherhead wouldn't let him leave the ship until he had paid back the crew. Jake had promised to reward each of them with a crate of crystals once they reached Altus, but they had been forced to leave empty-handed.

'It won't be the same without you,' said Jake.

'I'll be back before you know it.' Callidus checked the door and lowered his voice. 'But that's not why I wanted to talk.'

'What is it?' asked Jake. 'Did you find something else on the gunship?'

'Yes, I searched the Interstellar Navy server for the date you arrived on Remota and downloaded this audio file.'

Callidus held out a data crystal. Jake took the tiny sparkling disc and examined it.

'Does it have something to do with my dad's ship?'

'It's the captain's log.'

'You mean … ?'

'Yes,' said Callidus. 'It contains your father's last recorded words.'

Jake handled the data crystal as though it was a priceless treasure. Was he really holding his father's voice? He carefully slipped it into his computer and activated the device. His whole body shook with anticipation as he selected the audio file and pressed play.

'The Protectorate is not happy about this mission and neither is Amicus. He doesn't trust the Interstellar Navy, or anyone else for that matter. I just hope that Admiral Nex can protect our moons from the Galactic Trade Corporation.'

It was an old recording, which had become distorted over time. Jake struggled to make out the voice behind the interference, but it was definitely familiar. An eerie sensation washed over him. It was as though his father was speaking to him from beyond the grave.

'Apart from one or two last-minute changes, the crew has been hand-picked from the planetary guard.

It is Jake's first time in open space. Was I right to bring him along? Would it have been more dangerous to leave him behind? Here he is now. Say hello, Jake.'

There was a muffled noise that sounded like 'da-da-da.'

Jake's heart missed a beat. He was listening to himself talk eleven years ago aboard his father's ship. If only he could remember that precious moment. The recording hissed with static and skipped to a new entry.

'We've left behind the Tego Nebula and we're approaching the meeting point, not far from planet Remota. Amicus has the crew on alert and we're ready to defend ourselves if necessary.'

There was more static and then several explosions.

'We're under attack! If anyone is listening, our shields have failed and our weapons are not responding. I've ordered the crew to abandon ship. Amicus has taken Jake to Remota. I'm going to meet them there before we return to Altus, but there's no time to fetch the crown or sword. It had to be Kear, he must have –'

The audio file ended abruptly and the handheld computer fell silent. Jake stared at the screen, desperate to hear more, but he knew that it was the end. Moments later, his father had donned a spacesuit and thrown himself out of the airlock, before disappearing into an asteroid field.

Jake sat there, the words echoing in his head. The recording had confirmed everything that he already knew, but it had also raised more questions. How had Kear sabotaged the shields and weapons? Why had nobody checked the ship? What had stopped Jake's father from meeting them on Remota?

'Are you OK?' asked Callidus.

Jake looked up, unsure how he was feeling. 'Thanks for the recording. I know Granny Leatherhead would go mad if she found out you wasted time inside the gunship.'

'Don't worry about the captain, I can handle her,' said Callidus. 'Was it a waste of time?'

'No. It was strange to hear my dad talk, but it made him more real, if you know what I mean.' Jake rested his head in his hands. 'I've always had to imagine what he looks like, but at least I know what he sounds like, sort of.'

Callidus stroked his beard. 'Admiral Nex must have taken the recording from your father's ship before it was scrapped. That would explain why he was searching for Altus between Remota and the Tego Nebula, but without realising that you had come from inside the cloud itself. I wonder what else he took from that wreck.'

'Eleven years of my life,' said Jake, bitterly. 'Do you know which bit of that recording was the hardest to hear?'

Callidus shook his head.

'The silence at the end, because that's the moment I lost my dad.'

Without realising it, Jake pulled out his gold pendant and cupped it in his hands. The pendant was one of three unique items possessed by the rulers of Altus, along with a special crown and sword. Its round design and three precious stones represented Altus and its three crystal moons. Andras had given Jake the pendant as he abandoned ship and Jake had worn it ever since. He had recently discovered a picture inside of a beautiful albino woman with blood-red eyes. It was his mother, Zara Cutler, who had died giving birth to him.

'I can't change what has happened,' said Callidus. 'But if your father is still alive, I will help you to find him.'

'And how are you going to do that if you're not aboard this ship?' Jake unstrapped himself and stood up. 'Was there anything else?'

'There was one other thing that I managed to find out.' Callidus shifted uncomfortably. 'Kella's sister, Jeyne, has been transferred from a prison moon in the sixth solar system to Ur-Hal. It turns out that she was helping some United Worlds citizens to rebel against the Interstellar Government.'

'Jeyne was funding a rebellion?' said Jake in surprise. 'So we're not the only people who are fed-up with those pompous politicians. What is Ur-Hal?'

'It's a maximum-security prison planet in the first solar system,' said Callidus, his expression grim. 'There's no hope of saving her now. Once someone enters Ur-Hal, they never leave.'

Chapter 4

Shan-Ti Monastery

Callidus and Capio stood on the loading ramp, their travel bags slung over their shoulders. Beneath them, a string of docking bay lights glowed cold blue, making it seem as though they were about to enter a swimming pool. Nichelle had found a small outpost on the edge of the fifth solar system, where Callidus and Capio would be able to hitch a ride to visit the retired naval officer Helen Brack.

The crew gathered around the opening to see them off, including Kella, who stood silently with Nanoo. Jake had not told her about Jeyne yet. He wanted to wait for the right moment and they were rarely alone on the ship. It would not be an easy conversation. How do you tell someone that they will never see their sister again?

'Right, we had better be off,' announced Callidus, adjusting his bag.

'I can't believe that you're going,' said Jake. 'What if you can't find your buddy or she won't help us?'

'Then we'll be no worse off than we are now,' reasoned the fortune seeker. 'But it's worth a shot.'

'And what will we do if Admiral Vantard finds us?'

'You'll be OK,' said Callidus. 'We've evaded him for this long, haven't we? Wait for Capio and me at the monastery on Shan-Ti. We'll only be gone a few days.'

For the first time in months, the fortune seeker had a glint in his eye. He had even shaved off his beard, trimmed his nails and donned fresh clothes. It was as though he had a purpose again, a mission to accomplish, a reason to exist. Jake was glad to see the old Callidus back, but he hated to see him go, even for a few days. If it hadn't been for Callidus, Jake would not have made it off Remota, let alone discovered Altus. Space felt a lot safer when he was around. Jake would even miss curly-haired Capio and his incessant snoring.

'It's time to go,' said Granny Leatherhead, leaning on the bay wall. 'Before someone tries to arrest us, or worse, charge us a docking fee.'

Callidus nodded and winked at Jake. 'Just remember to keep an eye on the stars and stay out of trouble.'

With those words, he turned and trudged down the loading ramp, followed by Capio. Nichelle placed her arm around Jake as the two men disappeared into a cloud of condensation.

'Farid, close the ramp,' said Granny Leatherhead.

'Aye, captain.'

'Nichelle, fire up the engine.'

'Aye, captain.'

'As for the rest of you soppy sausages, you had better get yourselves strapped in for take-off. We've got a monastery to find.'

'Aye, captain.'

Jake lingered for a few seconds, his purple eyes scanning the blue mist below, hoping to catch another glimpse of Callidus and Capio. The ramp clamped shut and he was left staring at scuffed metal. Jake knew that he was being paranoid, but he couldn't help wondering if he would ever see the two of them again.

Shan-Ti was an independent colony in the fourth solar system. It reminded Jake of Remota with its jagged rocks and dusty surface, but instead of being dull and grey, the ground was a vibrant orange colour. This was intensified by the huge red sun that dominated the sky. Away from the towns and settlements, an old monastery had been carved into the wall of a giant crater, where the cyber-monks studied and worshipped technology. Its network of tunnelled corridors had only ever been seen by a handful of visitors. This now included the thirteen-year-old ruler of Altus.

'Let me get this straight,' said Father Benedict, his elbows perched on the edge of his stone desk. 'You're the teenage space pirate Jake Cutler, wanted by the Interstellar Navy. But you claim that it's all a misunderstanding and you were sent here by Father Pius Gates before he died.'

'Yes, that's right.'

Jake did his best to look sincere, while the cyber-abbot searched for signs of deception. It reminded Jake of when Callidus had met Father Pius on Remota, only this time it was Jake who was being scrutinised.

'You call destroying a naval warship a misunder-standing?' said Father Benedict. 'It's been a long time since anyone asked for sanctuary here. Don't get me wrong, we're not fond of the Interstellar Navy, but we don't want any trouble, especially not after what happened on Remota. If they discovered you here ...'

'It will only be for a few days, while my friends repair their ship,' promised Jake. 'We'll eat and sleep on the *Dark Horse*. You won't even know we're camped outside. We just need to borrow some of your tools and supplies.'

The cyber-abbot's office was similar to the one that Father Pius had occupied on Remota, except for the hazy red sunshine that flooded through the window. Its chiselled walls were covered with display screens and a small server hummed in the corner of the room. Father Benedict sat back in his black leather chair and stroked his neat white beard. His balding head glowed in the warm light, like a giant ruby egg in a nest of snowy white hair.

'And where are these friends of yours?' he asked. 'This crew of space pirates?'

'Not far from here,' said Jake. 'We wanted to avoid the space docks, so we landed in the shadows of the crater wall, which can be used as a launch pad when we leave. I know what you're thinking, but the Space Dogs are good people and they saved my life.'

The cyber-abbot rubbed his head studs while he reflected on the conversation. Jake knew that these special implants enabled cyber-monks to control computers with their thoughts.

'A few days?'

'That's all we need,' said Jake. 'We'll be gone before you know it. No one will ever know we were here.'

Father Benedict remained hesitant, perhaps afraid of breaking Interstellar Law.

'I was shocked to hear about the attack on Remota,' he said. 'Father Pius was a good friend; we studied together as novices. His death was a great loss to the order of Codos. All that work, gone forever.'

'What do you mean, gone?' asked Jake. 'I thought that cyber-monk research was uploaded to a secure server on the stellar-net.'

'Yes, most of it,' said the cyber-abbot. 'But Father Pius often worked on special projects for the cardinal. He would have saved any notes in files on his hand-held computer.'

Jake held up the device. 'You mean this one?'

Father Benedict caught sight of the smooth black device and his eyes widened. 'Is that Father Pius's?'

'Yes,' said Jake. 'He gave it to me when I left the monastery.'

'And you've had it all this time?'

'That's right, but I've not found any strange files or notes about special projects.'

'Incredible, absolutely incredible,' laughed Father Benedict. 'I don't know what would have happened if it had fallen into the wrong hands.'

Jake placed the device on the desk, but he kept his hand on it. 'Does this mean that we can stay?'

The Space Dogs were granted access to the monastery while Scargus and Manik repaired the *Dark Horse*; however, the cyber-monks were wary of strangers and they kept their distance. Jake tried several times to talk with the novices, hoping to borrow their technology to search for clues about his father, but they rushed off whenever he entered a room.

'It's funny,' he told Kella and Nanoo, as they took a walk around the crater. 'This place reminds me of the monastery on Remota, but at the same time it's completely different, like the universe changed when I wasn't looking.'

'Maybe it you who change,' said Nanoo.

'Perhaps, but it still feels weird to be treated like an outsider.' Jake rubbed his neck, wishing he had worn a hat. He felt hot and irritable in the midday sun.

'You had better get used to it,' said Kella. 'Not many people like space pirates.'

Kella was in a bad mood. Jake knew that she was missing her parents and she was worried about her sister. He wondered if it was the right moment to tell her about Jeyne. How would she react?

Nanoo fanned himself with his large hands. 'It shame cyber-monks take your handheld computer. What so special about files?'

'No idea,' said Jake. 'As far as I know, the brothers on Remota never discovered anything exciting.

Father Benedict has promised to return the device once he's removed any notes.'

Kella wiped her brow. 'How do people live in this heat?'

'I guess they don't go out much.' Jake glanced up at the huge red sun. 'Let's get back to the ship, before we start to cook out here.'

The three of them cut across the crater to the *Dark Horse* on the opposite side. Its new paintwork had been reduced to streaks of red by the acid shower. Jake hadn't appreciated how big the crater was, or how far they had walked. His tired feet scuffed on sharp rocks as they trudged across the dusty surface. He wondered how long they would be stuck on this rankful planet.

'Why does everything have to be so hard?' he grumbled. 'All I want to do is find my dad and lead a normal life. Is that too much to ask? I'm fed up of running and hiding while he's out there somewhere, waiting for me.'

'Maybe he hear about you on *Interstellar News* and he get in touch,' said Nanoo cheerfully.

'Yeah, maybe.' Jake forced himself to smile, but a voice in the back of his head kept repeating the same question over and over: *What if you never find him?*

'I keep thinking about Jeyne,' said Kella. 'If only we knew where they were keeping her. We could rescue her, like Wild Joe Jagger and the Ranko prison break.'

Jake peered into her hopeful eyes and knew it was time to tell her the truth. 'I'm sorry, but we can't help her.'

'Why not?'

'Your sister has been transferred to Ur-Hal.'

'What?' Kella looked confused. 'I don't understand.'

'Callidus told me that Jeyne has been transferred from a prison moon in the sixth solar system to Ur-Hal.'

Kella stopped walking. 'When did he tell you that?'

'Does it matter?' said Jake. 'I thought you had a right to know.'

'Ur-Hal?' Kella's eyes searched the air for answers. 'But that's a maximum-security prison planet. Why would they take her there?'

'According to Callidus, she was helping some United Worlds citizens to rebel against the Interstellar Government.'

'Garbish!' snapped Kella. 'My sister isn't a ... I mean, she wouldn't ... Jeyne, a rebel?'

'Perhaps she's tired of the lies and greed,' said Jake. 'And who could blame her? How many

51

politicians have been bribed by the Galactic Trade Corporation? It's just a pity that she was caught before her friends could take down the Interstellar Government.'

'But Ur-Hal?' Kella staggered backwards, holding her head and swaying in the heat. 'You promised to help me find her.'

'I know.'

'You hear stories ... only the most dangerous criminals are sent there ... I'll never see her again.'

Nanoo reached out and caught Kella as she stumbled on some rocks. Kella collapsed in his long arms, overwhelmed by the heat and the news.

'Come on,' said Jake, wrapping one of her arms around his shoulder, while Nanoo took the other. 'Let's get her back to the ship.'

Chapter 5

Trouble in the Seventh Solar System

'You can't hang about here all day, Jakey-boy,' said Scargus, prodding the contents of the hammock with his hammer.

'Why not?'

'Because I need to fix this old space tub and your miserable face is putting me off my work.'

Jake humphed. He had been skulking in the cluttered engine room since returning to the *Dark Horse*. His skin prickled with heat rash and he had a pounding headache. Kella was resting in her room while Nanoo watched over her. This was not a problem for Nanoo, because his people, the Novu, only slept once every three days.

'Here you go,' said Manik, holding out a steaming flask. 'I made you some pirate tea.'

Jake sat up and accepted the drink. 'Thanks.'

No one brewed a flask like Manik. It had been Manik who had taught Jake how to make pirate tea, using two teabags, three sugars and powdered milk in a gravity-proof flask. That seemed like a lifetime ago, before the black hole, before Altus, before his father's voice.

'Do you think I'll ever find my dad?' he asked.

'You underestimate yourself,' said Scargus, raising his bushy grey eyebrows, which looked like two tiny rainclouds. 'If anyone can find Andras Cutler, it's the teenage boy who located Altus and defeated his uncle.'

'I guess so,' sighed Jake, but it felt as though they were searching for a pin in a star cluster.

'Good,' said Scargus. 'Now cheer up and give me a hand.'

Jake reluctantly slid off the hammock on to the engine-room floor. He wasn't in the mood to recalibrate the rear shields, but it would help to take his mind off his father.

'How are the repairs going?' he asked.

'Not bad, not bad,' said Scargus, slipping the hammer into his tool belt. 'But it'll be a while until we can afford another paint job.'

'How are we paying for all the new parts?' asked Jake. 'I thought that we had no money for food, let alone anything else.'

'We're as skint as cyber-monks, if you pardon the expression.'

'Does that mean we're stealing the parts?'

'When have we had a chance to steal anything? Apart from the supplies we took off the naval gunship, we've been too busy running and hiding to do any proper spacejacking.' Scargus took off his glasses and wiped them on his crumpled cargo trousers. 'If you must know, the captain has sold her collection of fine dresses.'

'Her what?'

Jake had never seen Granny Leatherhead wear a skirt, let alone a fine dress. It seemed odd to imagine her in anything other than a combat suit.

'Lizzy might not wear dresses in space,' said Scargus, 'but she'll need something more respectable than pirate clothes when she retires.'

'And she's sold them?'

'Aye, at the trading station.'

'But I wouldn't mention it to her,' said Manik. 'It took the captain years to collect those dresses.'

No wonder Granny Leatherhead looked so cranky. Jake owed her and the crew a lot of crystals. How would he ever earn enough to pay them back without returning to Altus?

'Listen, Jake,' said Scargus. 'Your mind is clearly not on shield recalibration. Why don't you nip up to the dining area and fetch yourself some of that cyber-monk stew.'

Jake nodded and left the engine room, still clutching his pirate tea. He decided to check on Kella, but as he approached the guest quarters, she emerged from her room with Nanoo.

'Hey, Jake,' said Nanoo, his skin now dark lilac from the Shan-Ti sun. 'You not look good.'

'Thanks, mate. You look pretty bad yourself. How are you feeling, Kella?'

'How do you think?' she muttered, her eyes red and puffy.

'I'm sorry,' he said. 'I should have told you about Jeyne sooner.'

'Would it have made any difference?'

'No, I suppose not.'

'It's not your fault she's in Ur-Hal.' Kella rubbed her brow. 'Can I borrow your pendant? I need the crystals to heal my headache.'

It was the least that Jake could do. He slipped the gold chain over his head, but before he could hand it to Kella, the door to the cargo hold opened and Granny Leatherhead stepped out.

'What are you horrible lot up to?' she demanded.

The captain looked exhausted as she eyed them suspiciously. Her skin appeared yellow and blotchy in the dim corridor light.

'We're not up to anything,' said Jake, the pendant dangling from his hand.

'So why are you hanging about down here when there's work to be done? I don't care if you're an alien, a crystal healer or the ruler of Altus. No one gets special treatment aboard this ship.'

'Aye, captain,' said Jake.

'Now get your sunburnt butts –'

Granny Leatherhead stopped in mid-sentence and clasped her stomach with claw-like fingers. Her face contorted and she cried out with pain before collapsing on to the grated floor.

'Captain,' cried Jake, rushing to her side. 'What's wrong?'

Kella and Nanoo were close behind and helped to prop Granny Leatherhead up against the corridor wall.

'It hurts,' she wailed, holding her stomach. 'It's like I've been stabbed with a cutlass.'

'Let me take a look,' said Kella, lifting Granny Leatherhead's fingers and prodding her swollen belly. 'Is that tender?'

'Ouch!' shrieked the captain. 'Mind what you're poking, girl.'

Kella chewed her lip and studied Granny Leatherhead's gaunt, yellow face. 'Muscle pain, jaundiced skin and livid spots. I reckon you've got Kalos scurvy, captain.'

'What?'

'Kalos scurvy. It's quite common among space-farers, especially those who eat a poor diet. The first recorded case was on Kalos a hundred years ago, when a food shortage led to an outbreak and half the population died.'

Granny Leatherhead swallowed hard. 'Am I going to die?'

'Not if I can help it,' said Kella, putting aside her own problems. 'Jake, let me have your gold pendant.'

'Can you stop the pain?' asked Granny Leatherhead.

'I'm going to try,' said Kella, taking the pendant and holding it face down, so the crystals hovered over the swollen flesh.

'What we do?' asked Nanoo.

'Go and get a stretcher,' instructed Kella. 'We need to move the captain up to the medical bay.'

Kella stooped over Granny Leatherhead and moved her hand in determined patterns while the crystals glowed through her fingers. If anyone could save the captain, it was Kella. Her crystal healing talents had been used to help most of the crew since she had become the ship's medic.

Jake and Nanoo collected the stretcher from the medical bay and returned to the lower level. While they were gone Kodan and Woorak had joined Kella and the captain. Granny Leatherhead could barely keep her eyes open.

'W-w-will she be OK?' stuttered Woorak.

'Yes,' said Kella. 'I've reduced the swelling and eased the pain, but she's going to need plenty of rest, as well as fresh fruit and vegetables.'

'Rest?' moaned Granny Leatherhead. 'I can't rest. Who will look after the *Dark Horse*?'

'Farid can take charge,' said Jake. 'He is the first mate.'

Granny Leatherhead shook her head. 'I've not taken a day off sick in twenty years and I'm not starting now.'

The captain tried to stand, but her body had other ideas. With a cry of pain, she slid back down the wall and slumped on to the corridor floor.

'Do you want to make it to retirement?' asked Kella. 'If you don't rest, you won't make it off this planet.'

'OK, fine, I'll take it easy,' winced Granny Leatherhead. 'Whatever it takes.'

'Good.' Kella stood up. 'And stay off the rum.'

Granny Leatherhead grabbed hold of Kella's wrist and pulled her close. 'I owe you, girl. Who knows what would have happened to me if you hadn't been aboard this ship.'

Kella withdrew her arm and smiled modestly. 'I'll come and check on you later.'

Kodan and Woorak strapped the captain to the stretcher and carried her up to the medical bay on the second floor. As they disappeared from view, Jake heard the captain's voice echo down the corridor. 'Watch those stairs, you clumsy clowns.'

Nanoo looked appreciatively at Kella. 'Good work, ship medic.'

Kella half smiled, but her eyes remained sad.

'The crew is lucky to have you,' said Jake. 'I reckon that you've earned yourself a bowl of cyber-monk stew.'

The cyber-monks had shared some of their supplies with the crew, including a stew made with vegetables from the monastery gardens. Jake warmed up three portions before sitting down with Kella and Nanoo to eat in the dining area. He figured that it would make good comfort food and it might cheer Kella up. In the background, a wall display was set to the *Interstellar News*.

'Hey, turn it up,' said Kella, noticing a scrolling headline. 'It's about the Interstellar Navy.'

Jake read the words 'incident in the seventh solar system' and tapped the screen.

'... It's still not clear what the fleet of warships is doing in the seventh solar system,' said an energetic male reporter from the cockpit of his news craft. 'But the wreckage has been confirmed as a planetary guard vessel from the independent colony of Vantos.'

'Do we know who fired first?' asked the studio newsreader from a small window in the corner of the screen.

'The Interstellar Navy is claiming that the Vantos vessel launched an unprovoked attack,' said the reporter. 'However, the Vantos government is refusing to accept that their planetary guard would intentionally start a fight with a naval fleet. It could be the case that the Vantos ship fired by accident.'

'A malfunction?' asked the newsreader, raising an eyebrow. 'Or perhaps sabotage?'

'Anything is possible at this stage,' said the reporter. 'Vantos is famous for refusing to let the Galactic Trade Corporation mine its crystal-rich mountains. It could be that the Interstellar Navy is here to put pressure on the Vantos government.'

An image of the naval fleet appeared on the display, followed by a picture of a burnt-out wreck, which was little more than a blackened tangle of twisted metal.

'Does this count as an act of war?' asked the newsreader, placing a heavy emphasis on the last word.

'It's difficult to say until we know what really happened,' said the reporter. 'But with tensions rising between the United Worlds and the independent colonies, an incident like this could easily trigger a wider conflict.'

'Thanks, Tom.' The newsreader turned to face the camera as her window filled the screen. 'We'll bring you more on that story as it develops. It comes on the same day the Interstellar Government announced an alliance with the Gorks to form a special naval fleet. A spokesperson has described the deal as a major step forward in alien relations, creating thousands of jobs for unemployed Gorks. However, several independent colonies have criticised the Interstellar Government for arming a notoriously violent species while paying them half the minimum wage. In other news, the price of crystals continues to rise ...'

Jake tried to make sense of what they had heard. Why were there so many naval vessels in the seventh solar system?

'I don't like the sound of the Interstellar Navy joining forces with the Gorks,' said Kella. 'As if there aren't enough wretchards searching for us already.'

Jake agreed. 'We should tell the captain.'

'No, she needs to rest,' said Kella, firmly.

Maaka 'Metal Head' entered the dining area, accompanied by a nervous-looking novice from the monastery.

'Jake, you've got a visitor.'

The novice stood in front of the table, fidgeting with his white tunic. His expression was a mixture of fear and distaste as he stared at the glowing wall panels. Jake had seen him around the monastery, but like the other novices, he had kept his distance.

'Hello,' said Jake and the novice jumped. 'Did Father Benedict send you?'

'Yes, that's right. He wants to see you in his office.'

'Did he say why?'

'We've received a video message,' said the novice. 'It's for you.'

Jake, Kella and Nanoo followed the novice to the monastery, where they were led through the tunnelled corridors to the cyber-abbot's office. Father Benedict stood alone in front of a large display screen, his expression solemn.

'You had better take a seat,' he said, gesturing to three empty chairs. 'We received this video message about an hour ago, but it was encrypted and we've only just decoded it.'

The three of them sat down while Father Benedict used his skull implants to activate the display. Jake leant forward and watched eagerly as the screen lit up.

'It Callidus and Capio,' said Nanoo.

Jake was glad to see that the two men were OK. Father Benedict dimmed the lights and started the video.

'Ahoy, Shan-Ti monastery,' said Callidus. 'This is a message for Jake Cutler.'

Callidus sat closest to the camera, while Capio pottered in the background. It was strange to see them squeezed into the flickering display, their distorted voices carried across the stars on the stellar-net.

'Jake, I wanted to let you know that we've found my old navy buddy,' said the fortune seeker. 'I'll get straight to the point: Helen doesn't think that any planet or spaceport will be safe for you and the crew, not since the ISS Colossus disappeared. It sounds as though we've really shaken the Interstellar Navy. There are also rumours that the Galactic Trade Corporation is running out of crystals, which is why they're so keen to find Altus and drill its moons. A crystal shortage would be disastrous for the United Worlds.'

Capio mumbled something about missing the opportunity of a lifetime. Callidus ignored him and leant closer to the camera.

'Helen suspects that the Interstellar Government needs crystals to fund a war against the independent colonies, wiping them out forever. Admiral Vantard is trying to convince people that the colonies are plotting to attack the United Worlds, but this is an excuse to strengthen his fleet and strike first. If he succeeds, it could affect every single planet in the seven solar systems. In short, he will start the first ever galactic war.'

Jake nearly slipped off his chair. Galactic war? He wondered if he had misheard, but an alarmed look from Kella confirmed that he had not. Father Benedict muttered something and shook his head.

'Listen, try not to worry,' said Callidus. 'It's not as if Admiral Vantard or the Galactic Trade Corporation are close to finding Altus. Helen believes that there's still time for negotiations. But I thought you should know what Admiral Vantard is planning. It's essential that he never finds those crystal moons, which is why you and the crew should remain on Shan-Ti for as long as possible.'

Callidus paused for a moment and Jake wondered if it was the end of the message.

'There's something else,' said the fortune seeker, looking away from the camera. 'Helen told me something that I wasn't expecting. As you know, I don't remember much before the Interstellar Navy, only that they found me in a canteen. Until now, I didn't even know the name of the planet. Helen has shared that information and she reckons that it's time I confronted my past.'

Callidus took a long breath and stared into the camera. 'And I think she's right. I've always wondered about my lost memories, despite never having the courage to search for them. I might not like what I find, but you've inspired me, Jake. You were brave enough to work out who you were and where you were from, so I'm going to do the same. Who knows, maybe I'll discover what my head studs are for.'

Jake had once asked Callidus about the two metal lumps fixed to his temples. He'd wondered if they were similar to the skull implants used by the cyber-monks to control computers. Callidus had no idea what his studs were for, but it sounded as though he was going to find out.

'Good for you,' said Capio, patting his friend on the shoulder.

Callidus smiled. 'It means that Capio and I will be heading to the seventh solar system, instead of joining you on Shan-Ti. I don't know how long it will take to get some answers – perhaps a few days. I know you'll understand why I need to do this, Jake. If you leave the planet, ask the cyber-monks to forward my messages. In the meantime, remember to keep an eye on the stars and stay out of trouble.'

The video message ended and Father Benedict turned off the display. Jake was sitting back in his chair, trying to take in the message, when something struck him.

'The seventh solar system,' he said. 'Callidus and Capio are heading straight for the naval fleet.'

Chapter 6

The Mayor of Remota

'We have to warn them,' said Jake. 'We have to stop Callidus and Capio from entering the seventh solar system.'

'How?' asked Nanoo. 'We not know where they going, so how we send message?'

Jake groaned. Nanoo was right; they had no idea which planet Callidus and Capio were visiting. He hoped that the two men had seen the *Interstellar News* and stayed clear.

'What about the independent colonies?' Kella looked at Jake with expectant eyes.

'What about them?'

'You need to let the leaders know what's happening.'

'Me?' choked out Jake. 'I can't just contact the independent colony leaders.'

'Why not?' she said. 'You're one of them, aren't you?'

'As far as everyone is concerned, I'm just a teen-age space pirate. Why would they listen to me?

What proof do I have that the Interstellar Navy is trying to fund a war?'

'It explain why there is navy fleet over Vantos,' said Nanoo. 'To take crystals from mountains.'

'I bet that's the real reason they arrested Jeyne.' Kella scowled. 'So they could get their hands on my family's crystal mine.'

Father Benedict cleared his throat. Jake had almost forgotten that he was still in the room.

'I don't know what your friend meant about Altus,' said the cyber-abbot. 'But if there's the slightest possibility of a galactic war, we should do everything within our power to stop it, or risk having the blood of millions on our hands. It will be too late once the Interstellar Navy strengthens its fleet.'

Jake's mouth fell open. 'Gorks.'

'I'm sorry?'

'It was on the *Interstellar News* just now.' Jake slapped his forehead. 'The Interstellar Navy has signed an alliance with the Gorks to strengthen its fleet. Don't you see? It's already too late.'

The truth spread around the room like an acid shower. Admiral Vantard no longer needed crystals. He must have promised the Gorks something in return for their support. Perhaps a planet of their own, if they helped to wipe out the independent colonies, starting with Vantos. The seventh solar system was where the galactic war would start.

'Jake, you have to warn the independent colony leaders,' said Kella.

'How?' asked Jake. 'The only politicians I know are hiding back on Altus.'

'Is there nobody else?'

'What about leaders here on Shan-Ti?' suggested Nanoo.

'And let them know that a crew of wanted space-jackers is hiding on their planet?' Jake stood up and paced the room.

The idea that someone wanted to wipe out the independent colonies seemed too incredible to be true. Whole planets were in danger, but what could he do about it? If only he knew someone on Vantos, or Reus, or Remota …

'That's it,' he said, turning to Father Benedict. 'Is there any way to contact another planet without giving away our location?'

'You mean a video message?'

'No, we don't have time to send messages,' said Jake. 'I want to speak with someone in real time, like a phone call.'

The cyber-abbot looked around the room for inspiration and spotted clusters of thick rubber cables climbing the walls. 'We have several powerful satellites, which are normally used to download data from the stellar-net. These could be used to access another planet's phone network.'

'Great. How quickly can you set it up?'

'I don't know, we've never had to call anyone off-world before. Let me speak with the brothers.'

'Who do you want to contact?' asked Kella.

'The mayor of Remota,' said Jake. 'I met him once when the cyber-monks fixed a computer virus in his office. He's not as influential as the president of Reus, but he's the best I can come up with right now.'

Jake, Kella and Nanoo returned to the *Dark Horse* to check on the captain. When they reached the medical bay, the hatch door was open. Granny Leatherhead limped out, supported by Kodan. Her long leather coat hung from her frail shoulders.

'Where are you going?' asked Kella.

'To the bridge, where I belong,' said Granny Leatherhead. 'I can't sleep in that wretched room. It stinks of antiseptic.'

Kella folded her arms and spoke firmly. 'You need to rest. If you can't sleep in the medical bay, then

I suggest you lie down in your quarters. It's for your own good. We can bring you some pirate tea and cyber-monk stew.'

Granny Leatherhead humphed. Not many people would get away with bossing around the captain on her own ship. But to Jake's surprise, the old pirate hobbled off to her quarters.

'Captain, wait,' he said, chasing after her. 'You need to know something.'

Granny Leatherhead stopped outside her black hatch door on the top deck. 'What is it, Kid Cutler?'

Jake told her about the video message and how the Interstellar Navy had joined forces with the Gorks. 'If Admiral Vantard attacks the independent colonies, it could lead to a galactic war.'

Granny Leatherhead shrugged. 'Why should I care if the United Worlds and independent colonies want to kill each other? At least that would keep the Interstellar Navy off our backs for a while.'

The captain shuffled into her quarters and closed the door. Jake stood there for a moment, unsure what to make of her reaction. He hoped that the mayor of Remota would be more concerned by the news. Jake, Kella and Nanoo made their way to the dining area on the first deck, where they found Scargus rummaging through some empty containers.

'Hello, shipmates,' said the engineer. 'I heard about the captain collapsing. Is it true that she's got Kalos scurvy?'

'Yes, that's right,' confirmed Kella.

Scargus whistled. 'Poor Lizzy, it was only a matter of time before her body started to complain. It's a good job you three were there to help.'

There was a loud cough behind them. Jake turned to find Father Benedict standing by the door.

'Hello,' said the cyber-abbot. 'Forgive the intrusion, but the loading ramp was open.'

Jake was pleased to see him. 'Is it ready?'

'We've been able to connect our satellites to the phone network on Remota. Not only that, but the brothers have found a way to patch it through to your handheld computer.' Father Benedict held out the device. 'Are you ready to prevent a galactic war?'

'What did you say?' Scargus almost dropped a food container.

'We'll explain later,' said Kella.

Jake took the device. 'Have you removed all of the research files?'

The cyber-abbot nodded. 'We found some useful notes and calculations, but not as much as we had hoped. At least none of it fell into the wrong hands.

I thought you might like the device back for sentimental reasons. No one should be able to trace any calls or e-comms from it.'

Jake took the handheld computer. He had expected it to look different somehow, but it was still the same device that Father Pius had given him on Remota.

'Thank you,' he said. 'I'll do everything I can to stop the Interstellar Navy, you have my word.'

Jake slipped into one of the seats and activated the computer, while the others gathered around. He located the contact details for the mayor of Remota and tapped the screen to connect. There was a brief delay before the device let out an electronic purr.

'Hello?' answered a deep, rich voice.

'Is that Hector Rumpole?' asked Jake, picturing a bumbling man with a bulbous nose, walrus moustache and ruddy cheeks. 'The mayor of Remota?'

'Yes, that's right. How can I help?'

'I don't know if you remember me – my name is Jake Cutler.'

'Great gubbins!' exclaimed the mayor. 'Are you that purple-eyed orphan who lived with the cyber-monks? I thought that you were killed when the monastery burned down. What a terrible ordeal, blasted spacejackers. You sound far away; where are you?'

'Further than you think,' said Jake. 'I'm calling to warn you about the Interstellar Navy. There's no easy way of saying this, but they are preparing to attack the independent colonies, starting with the seventh solar system.'

'What are you talking about? Not even the Interstellar Navy is stupid enough to want a galactic war.'

'That's exactly what they want,' said Jake. 'It's why they've formed an alliance with the Gorks. We have to warn the other leaders and unite the independent colonies before it's too late.'

'Warn the other … unite the …' spluttered Hector Rumpole. 'Is this your idea of a joke, Jake Cutler? The whole galaxy is tense enough already with naval warships surrounding Vantos. Now is the time for diplomacy, not fantasy.'

'It's no joke,' insisted Jake. 'You have to listen to me. I'm also a leader, the ruler of an independent colony.'

'Oh, really?' said the mayor. 'Which one?'

Jake hesitated, realising how ridiculous the truth sounded, but it was too late to change his story.

'Altus.'

'I see.' Hector Rumpole spoke quietly, but Jake could detect anger in his voice.

'I'm not lying.'

'That's funny, I must have missed the discovery of Altus on the *Interstellar News*,' said the mayor. 'Was it after they announced that crystals are really space pixie eggs? Next you'll tell me that you're the teenage space pirate we've been hearing so much about. I would love to know the location of this mythical planet that has made you its ruler.'

'I can't tell you; it's a secret.'

'How convenient. I suppose it's too much to hope that the Altian people gave you a crown, or something else to prove that your story is anything other than utter garbish?'

'The crown was lost, along with the sword, but I have a pendant, or rather a locket –'

'Goodbye, Jake.'

There was a loud click, followed by the electronic purr, as the mayor of Remota ended the call. Jake stared at the handheld computer, waiting for it to do something.

'That not good,' said Nanoo.

Jake buried his head in his hands. 'That was a disaster.'

'Don't give up,' said Kella. 'You have to make people listen.'

'How? You heard him, he thinks that I'm a liar. Would you believe me if you hadn't seen Altus for yourself?'

'It's a pity you don't have a crown, or that special sword you told me about,' said Scargus. 'A golden cutlass would make most people stop and listen.'

Jake thought about this for a moment. 'Yes, it would.'

'What on your mind, Jake?' asked Nanoo.

'We have to find the missing crown and sword of Altus. I already have the seal of Altus and the uniform of a ruler. If I had the crown and sword as well, Hector Rumpole would have to take me seriously.'

Kella peered at him through narrowed eyes. 'I thought they were lost when your father's ship was destroyed.'

'They were, but someone must know what happened to them,' said Jake. 'And I know who we can ask.'

Scargus eyed him curiously. 'Who?'

'The last person to see the wreckage,' said Jake. 'The salvage captain, Baden Scott.'

It had been an hour since Father Benedict had left the ship. Jake was on the handheld computer, trying to track down Baden Scott's salvage trawler, the *Rough Diamond III*. Kella had gone to check on Granny Leatherhead, while Scargus had returned to the engine room to finish the repairs. Nanoo was in the monastery with the cyber-monks, seeing if their satellites were powerful enough to send a message back to Taan-Centaur. Jake suspected that Nanoo might offer to boost the signal.

'Magnifty,' he shouted, sitting up and staring at his device. 'I've got you.'

Jake hurried up the metal staircase to the captain's quarters. He wasn't sure what he was going to say, but he needed her permission to launch the ship. As he reached the top deck, he saw Kella standing outside the black hatch door.

'What's going on?' she asked.

'I've found him,' said Jake. 'I've tracked down Baden Scott. His salvage trawler is docked at a service port in the sixth solar system.'

'That's great – so what happens now?'

'We go and speak to him.'

'You mean leave Shan-Ti?' said Kella. 'I don't know if the captain is ready for space flight.'

'I'm sorry, but I have to prove that I'm the ruler of Altus before the Interstellar Navy attacks Vantos.'

Jake went to step past her, but Kella blocked the door.

'You're not listening to me,' she said. 'Space travel puts a strain on the body and the captain needs to rest.'

'And millions will die if we stay here,' said Jake. 'We'll have to leave the captain with the cyber-monks.'

The hatch door slid open with a mechanical hiss. Granny Leatherhead stood in the doorway, scowling. In spite of her weakened state, she was still the most frightening person that Jake had ever met.

'Are you going somewhere, Kid Cutler?' she asked. 'And who are you leaving behind?'

'We need to launch the ship,' he said. 'I have to warn the independent colony leaders about the Interstellar Navy, but no one will listen to me without the crown and sword of Altus. Baden Scott is in the sixth solar system. He mentioned a golden sword the first time we met and he might know what happened to the crown.'

Granny Leatherhead rubbed her forehead. 'I've told you before, I don't care if the United Worlds and independent colonies destroy each other. I expect there's good money to be made from war.'

'Money?' Kella looked horrified. 'Why is it always about money? Millions of people could suffer and die. Where will you spend your retirement fund if the independent colonies get wiped out? There will be no more Shan-Ti, no more Remota, no more Reus.'

Granny Leatherhead regarded Kella with a weary eye, her expression unfathomable.

'I'll give you the sword,' said Jake. 'If you help us to prevent a galactic war, I'll give you the sword of Altus. It must be worth a fortune, more than the crystals I owe you.'

'You'll give me a golden cutlass?' Granny Leatherhead raised an eyebrow. 'That sounds very generous, but how do I know it's not the size of my finger?'

'When we were on Altus, I saw paintings of past rulers wearing the crown and holding the sword,' said Jake. 'It's the same size as any other cutlass, except it's pure gold and encrusted with jewels. Do we have a deal?'

Jake spat on his hand and held it out. Granny Leatherhead took a moment to consider the offer and then shook his hand.

'OK, it's a deal. I'll help you to save the galaxy in return for the sword,' she said, before pulling him closer so he could feel her foul breath on his face. 'And if you ever think about leaving me behind again, I'll chop off your legs and feed them to Kodan.'

Chapter 7

Admiral Voratio Vantard

'What going on?' asked Nanoo, entering the engine room. 'Why is crew packing up ship?'

'We're taking off as soon as we finish the repairs,' said Jake, who was helping Scargus to replace a damaged shield generator. 'How did you get on with the cyber-monk satellites?'

'It hard to say,' sighed Nanoo. 'We send message to Taan-Centaur, but Father Benedict say it take one week to reach there, let alone reply.'

Nanoo muttered something in his own language – a mixture of disappointed clicks and whistles.

'At least your people will know what happened to you and your parents,' said Jake.

'I suppose you right. It give me hope that I see Taan-Centaur again one day.'

Jake understood what it was like to be far away from home. He had never felt so unsettled, so unanchored, so adrift. His father had been missing since he was two years old. When the monastery on Remota

82

was destroyed and the cyber-monks were killed, Jake's only chance for a normal life seemed to be on Altus, but he had abandoned that planet to search for his father. Now he was on the run from the Interstellar Navy and every fortune seeker in the galaxy as the most wanted space pirate in the seven solar systems with a bounty on his head and nowhere to call home. How had things gone so wrong?

All his hopes rested on finding Andras Cutler. Jake hadn't considered what would become of him if he couldn't locate his father. Was he destined to be alone, skulking in the shadows like a common criminal? His father's friend, Amicus Kent, had gone from being a top Altian general to a space hobo, before dying in a service port canteen. Jake had to find his father, whatever it took, but even that would have to wait until they had saved the seven solar systems.

Nanoo helped Scargus and Jake to connect the shield generator while Manik checked the engine. Squawk, the ship's foul-mouthed parrot, flew in circles above their heads, screeching insults.

'Fish face, potty pants, butt brains.'

'Where does he learn those words?' asked Jake.

'Granny Leatherhead, mostly,' said Scargus, standing back and wiping his hands. 'There, that should do the trick.'

'You fix everything?' asked Nanoo.

Scargus shook his head. 'Not quite; only the important stuff, like the shields and the worst of the acid damage.'

'I'll tell Nichelle to prepare for take-off,' said Manik.

Jake and Nanoo headed to the guest quarters to strap themselves in. It had been a while since the *Dark Horse* had launched from a planet surface. If their escape from Altus was anything to go by, it was going to be rough. Jake had moved into the same room as Nanoo and Kella while Callidus and Capio were away. Any worries about sharing with a girl and an alien had soon been forgotten, when the three of them spent the first night making up space shanties instead of sleeping.

Inside the room, they found Kella sitting on her bunk, her arms wrapped around her knees.

'Are you OK?' asked Jake.

'No,' she said, without looking.

'That's what I figured.' Jake kicked off his gravity boots and climbed into his bed. 'I know you're still upset about your sister. If there's anything I can do ... anything ... ?'

'I want you to destroy the Interstellar Navy,' she said bitterly. 'I want you to unite the independent colonies and destroy the Interstellar Navy.'

Jake didn't respond at first, because he wasn't sure if Kella was being serious. He watched a tear escape from her eye and trickle down her cheek.

'I thought we try to prevent galactic war,' said Nanoo. 'Not start one.'

'Why not attack?' Kella's expression hardened. 'My sister was trying to take down the Interstellar Government. If she can betray the United Worlds, why can't I?'

'Because millions of people will die,' said Jake.

Kella hung her head. 'But what else can I do? The only way to get Jeyne out of Ur-Hal is to destroy the Interstellar Navy. I just want my sister back.'

Jake didn't respond. Kella was angry and it would only make things worse to argue with her. The three of them sat in silence, listening to the distant hum of the engine, when the intercom speakers crackled to life.

'Listen up, everyone, we're launching the ship in two minutes,' squeaked Farid like an excited mouse. 'Blast it, Scargus, hurry up and fix this wretched thing.'

Jake fastened his straps and counted down the seconds. It would be good to get away from the heat of Shan-Ti and back into open space. He pressed his hand against the wall and felt the hull vibrate as the engine grew louder. The amber ceiling light was broken in Kella's room, but Jake could still hear the siren wailing in the corridor. His heart beat faster and he braced himself for take-off.

'Here we go,' he shouted, as the exhausts blasted the crater wall.

The *Dark Horse* nudged forward, scraping along a temporary wooden jetty that Maaka and Woorak had constructed. Jake watched the evening sky pass by the porthole window as the ship gathered speed and left the ground. The force of acceleration pinned him to his mattress and pulled at his sweaty cheeks. He had missed the thrill of the launch. It was the most exciting sensation in the universe.

The old cargo hauler climbed steadily higher into the sky, until it escaped the planet's atmosphere. When Jake felt the temperature drop and his body lighten, he unclipped his bed straps and floated free from his bunk. Kella and Nanoo released their straps and joined him in the air. Jake pushed himself into the centre of the room and turned a double somersault.

'That nothing,' said Nanoo, holding on to the top bunk. 'Watch this.'

Nanoo kicked off with his legs and performed three perfect backflips before landing on the ceiling. Kella cheered and applauded.

'Nice one, Nanoo,' said Jake. 'At least you can move better than you can sing.'

'What you mean?'

'Sorry, Nanoo, but your space shanties are pretty jabberish,' said Kella. 'None of them make any sense.'

'Oh, I don't know,' laughed Jake. 'I liked the one about life as a spice parrot, or was that supposed to be space pirate? It made me –'

Jake's voice was drowned out by the ship's alarm.

'Battle stations,' said Farid, through the faulty intercom, his voice scratchy and warped. 'Maaka, Woorak, roll out the laser cannon.'

'Interstellar Navy?' wondered Nanoo. 'Or fortune seeker?'

Jake scrambled to the porthole window. 'There's nothing on this side.'

'Let's get to the bridge,' said Kella, plucking her gravity shoes off the wall.

The three of them hurried to the top deck, where Farid, Kodan and Nichelle were dressed in their pirate combat suits, complete with padded gloves, kit belts and silver skull-shaped space helmets. Jake spotted a large vessel through the front window, but it wasn't a naval warship or fortune seeker.

'What's going on?' he asked. 'Is that a spaceliner?'

'You bet your bones it is,' said Farid, rubbing his hands. 'We're going to spacejack it.'

'No,' protested Kella. 'We can't.'

'Why not?' Farid seemed taken aback. 'That's what we do; we're spacejackers.'

'The captain needs to rest,' said Kella.

'And we've got to find Baden Scott,' added Jake.

'I'm sorry,' said Farid. 'But we can't keep this ship running on promises.'

Jake watched the luxury spaceliner on a display screen, alone and vulnerable. Despite being aboard a pirate ship for three months, he had never witnessed a real spacejacking. It was one thing to steal supplies from a naval gunship, but it felt wrong to attack innocent people. How would he like it if someone took his gold pendant?

'What if *Dark Horse* get damaged?' asked Nanoo.

'We've been doing this for years,' boasted Farid. 'I think we can handle a lone spaceliner.'

'We're within firing range,' said Nichelle.

Kodan opened the panel beneath the main display and squeezed into the secret compartment, ready to unleash his multi-barrelled laser cannon on the unsuspecting ship.

'Stand by to reveal our colours,' instructed Farid, his eyes fixed on the main display.

'We're being hailed,' said Nichelle.

Farid laughed. 'Let me guess: they want to know our intentions?'

'It's not the spaceliner.' Nichelle spun around in her seat. 'We're being hailed by Admiral Vantard. He wants to speak with Captain Cutler.'

Farid dived across the bridge to check the scanners. 'It's the *ISS Magnificent*. Turn this ship about, full speed away.'

Nanoo fiddled with a display screen and located the naval warship. It hurtled towards them with its mighty laser cannon and huge launch locks. There was a time when Jake would have given anything to see such a powerful ship in space, but now it only filled him with dread. No wonder the spaceliner didn't need weapons; it was travelling with the finest warship in the Interstellar Navy. Farid had been too busy playing captain to check the long-range scanner.

'The *ISS Magnificent* is preparing to fire,' warned Nichelle. 'We're still in range, what do we do?'

Farid stiffened. 'I … I don't know.'

'We give them everything we've got, by Zerost,' barked a voice in the doorway.

Jake turned to see Granny Leatherhead holding on to the hatch frame, her silver hair hanging in straggles over her floral nightgown.

'Captain,' exclaimed Kella. 'What are you doing out of bed?'

Granny Leatherhead ignored her. 'Kodan, introduce those naval numpties to Old Lizzy.'

Kodan squeezed the trigger, releasing a torrent of laser bolts from the nose of the ship. Jake watched as they exploded against the warship's shields, but the *ISS Magnificent* held its course.

'Nichelle, give me your best evasive moves,' said Granny Leatherhead. 'I want to make Admiral Fancy-Pants feel space sick just watching us.'

'Aye, captain.'

'And what are the rest of you idiots waiting for?' Granny Leatherhead grabbed the intercom. 'Maaka, Woorak, target any naval fighters that poke their heads out of the launch locks. Scargus, Manik, squeeze every watt of power you can from the engine.'

'Aye, captain.'

'What about us?' asked Kella.

'Don't you know by now?' Granny Leatherhead shuffled over to the captain's chair. 'Kella, wait in the medical bay. Nanoo, keep the shields working.'

'Aye, captain.'

'Do you want me in the engine room?' asked Jake.

'No, not this time,' she said. 'I need you here. It's you he's asking for, not me.'

Kella and Nanoo rushed off to their posts, leaving Jake on the bridge. Granny Leatherhead thrust the communicator into his hand as the ship twisted and turned like a rickety rollercoaster.

'Well?' she said. 'Distract him.'

Jake held the communicator to his mouth. 'Ahoy, naval warship?'

'Ahoy, pirate scum,' said a loud, confident voice. 'This is Admiral Voratio Vantard of the righteous *ISS Magnificent*, ordering you to cut your engine and surrender immediately.'

Jake tried to think how Granny Leatherhead would respond to such a demand. 'This is Captain Cutler, of the *Dark Horse* cargo hauler. I'm sorry, but it's not in a space pirate's nature to surrender without a fight.'

Admiral Vantard let out a sharp laugh. 'I was hoping you would say that. I'm not afraid of you, Kiddie Cutler. You might be the most dangerous pirate of all time, but someone has to make you pay for murdering Admiral Nex and his crew.'

'It wasn't murder,' said Jake. 'The *ISS Colossus* attacked us and then it got sucked into a black hole.'

'Do you spacejackers ever tell the truth? Naval warships don't just stumble into black holes. I'm going to make you pay for every single trooper you killed.'

'Oh yeah?' Jake tried his best to sound like a ruthless pirate captain. 'If you don't turn your ship around, I'll destroy you as well.'

'Give me your best shot, boy,' said the admiral. 'I love it when space pirates fight back.'

The *ISS Magnificent* opened fire with its massive cannon, narrowly missing the *Dark Horse* with a string of barrel-sized laser bolts and flooding the bridge with light.

'Faster, Nichelle,' croaked Granny Leatherhead. 'We need to outrun that warship before it locks on to our rusty rivets.'

'I'm trying, captain,' said the pilot. 'Just give me a minute.'

'We don't have a minute,' snapped Granny Leatherhead, holding on to her stomach.

Jake realised that the captain was still suffering and she had sent Kella to the medical bay to get her out of the way. If the *Dark Horse* was going down, Granny Leatherhead wanted to be on the bridge, not strapped to a bed.

Kodan stopped firing Old Lizzy to leave more power for the engine. It wasn't much use having a laser cannon at the front of the ship when the enemy was behind them. Maaka and Woorak also struggled to get a clear shot with the side cannon.

'Captain.' Farid looked up from his scanners. 'I've picked up another craft heading straight for us.'

'Another warship?'

'No, it's a star frigate,' said Farid. 'It's the *Divine Wind*.'

'What?' Granny Leatherhead limped over to the scanners. 'Well, well, it looks like the crew survived their last encounter with Admiral Vantard and they fancy another go.'

Jake squinted at the front window and spotted the scorched yellow hull of the *Divine Wind* hurtling towards them, its pink laser cannon stretched out like fingers.

'It's going to ram us,' said Nichelle.

'Hold your course,' instructed Granny Leatherhead. 'If those pirates wanted to scupper us, they would have done so by now.'

Jake watched the *Divine Wind* storm towards them and pull up at the last second. It shot over their heads with a playful spin, passing so close that Jake was surprised not to hear the hull scrape. He turned to the main display and saw the star frigate fly straight into the path of the *ISS Magnificent*, its lasers blasting.

'That crew has a death wish,' said Granny Leatherhead.

The *Divine Wind* circled the naval warship like an insect bothering a wild animal. What did the blood-red letter 'K' stand for? Jake could only think of one pirate crew starting with a 'K', the Killer Kings, but they flew a white space clipper and they were rarely seen outside of the third solar system. It felt odd to be in the debt of a mysterious ship.

Granny Leatherhead looked ready to collapse as the *Dark Horse* made its escape. Farid tried to assist her, but she shrugged off his arm. The first mate had messed up and it had nearly cost the lives of the crew. Farid was lucky that Granny Leatherhead was so weak; otherwise he would not have still been standing. Kodan emerged from his compartment and held on to the captain's arm as she hobbled from the bridge.

'Where now?' asked Nichelle.

'The sixth solar system,' said Farid grumpily. 'But this time don't stop for anything.'

Chapter 8

The Captain's Daughter

It had been several hours since leaving Shan-Ti and there was no further sign of the Interstellar Navy. Jake had finished his engine-room chores and he was now lying on his bed, making up space shanties to pass the time. Kella sat on her bunk, using the handheld computer to browse medical sites, while Nanoo performed zero gravity acrobatics.

Jake sang them his latest song:

> *'Brave captain and hardy crew,*
> *Blast this ship into the black,*
> *Hey ho, to adventures new,*
> *Full thrust ahead and attack.*
> *Let me feel a blade of steel,*
> *And a laser in my hand,*
> *Raiding ships, plunder and steal,*
> *Only dead men dare to stand.'*

Kella peered over the top of the screen. 'Only dead men dare to stand?'

'Yeah,' said Jake. 'It's piratey, like in the stories.'

'I've not read many pirate tales,' she sniffed. 'I prefer stories about magic.'

'Well, I thought it magnifty,' said Nanoo. 'You good with songs, Jake.'

'Thanks, matey.'

'Why do they always have to be about spacejacking?' asked Kella. 'You should make one up about helping people.'

'What, a space shanty about crystal healing?'

'Why not?' she said. 'It would be a change to blood and treasure.'

Jake admired Kella's talent with crystals, but he doubted it would make a very good pirate song.

'How come you don't sing any more?' he asked. 'Your voice is, you know, beautiful.'

It was difficult to tell who was more embarrassed by this statement, Jake or Kella. She ducked behind the handheld computer, so only the top of her head could be seen.

'I only sing when I'm alone,' she said. 'I don't like people hearing me.'

'Why not?' asked Nanoo.

'I get embarrassed.' Kella lowered the device, but kept her mouth covered. 'Jeyne used to enter me for competitions, but I hated the thought of singing while strangers stared at me.'

The hatch door slid open and Maaka 'Metal Head' entered.

'Hello, Space Pups.'

Jake hated it when the crew called them that.

'What up, Maaka?' asked Nanoo.

'The captain wants to see you lot in her quarters.'

'Why?' asked Jake.

'You'll find out when you get there.'

Jake had never been inside the captain's quarters. Maaka led them up to the top deck and knocked on the black hatch door.

'Enter,' said a muffled voice.

The door opened, releasing wisps of fragrant incense. Jake stepped inside a wide cabin with two large porthole windows that overlooked the rear exhausts. The walls were decorated with star charts and a pair of crossed cutlasses. There was also a tarnished brass plaque displaying the ship's name. A large desk was fixed to the floor beside a model of the seven solar systems. In the corner of the room stood an empty cabinet, which Jake assumed had once contained a collection of fine dresses.

The low ceiling was bolstered by thick metal pillars, each wrapped with the flag of Zerost. Scargus had told Jake about the ice planet and how the Galactic Trade Corporation had abandoned it, forcing the starving colonists to become space pirates to survive. It turned out that Jake's ancestors, the crew that discovered Altus, were from Zerost, which meant that spacejacking was in his blood.

'Thank you, Maaka,' said Granny Leatherhead, who was strapped into a curved wooden bed. 'That will be all.'

The metal-faced shipmate nodded and left the room, leaving Jake, Kella and Nanoo with the captain. Jake spotted a needle and thread in her hand. He smiled at the thought of the tough old captain embroidering patches for the crew. It made her seem much less scary. He noticed a photo above her bed of a woman holding a baby, who looked like a younger and prettier version of Granny Leatherhead, only without the eyepatch.

'It's going to take us a couple of days to reach the sixth solar system and find Baden Scott,' said the captain. 'I want you to use that time wisely, because we don't know what will be waiting for us. The word on the stars is that Admiral Vantard is on the move and searching for something.'

'Us?' guessed Jake.

'Aye, probably.'

'I could contact my parents,' said Kella. 'I'm sure they could tell us what's happening in the sixth solar system.'

Granny Leatherhead scratched her crusty leather eyepatch. 'A nice idea, but it's not worth the risk.'

'But –'

'No arguments,' said the captain. 'I know you miss your family, but the Interstellar Navy will have been monitoring communications with your parents since the space mafia kidnapped you. It wouldn't surprise me if Papa Don has told them that you're now aboard the *Dark Horse*.'

'So what are we going to do?' asked Jake.

'We need a rear weapon,' said Granny Leatherhead. 'Old Lizzy and the side cannon are no use when we're attacked from behind. If it hadn't been for the *Divine Wind*, we would all be dead by now.'

'But where we find new laser cannon in space?' asked Nanoo.

'You see that?' Granny Leatherhead pointed to a narrow ladder between the porthole windows. 'It leads up to a hidden turret above the exhausts, but the laser cannon has been broken for years. Nanoo,

I want you to fix it, before taking over Jake's responsibilities in the engine room.'

'Aye, captain.'

'Kella, I want you to keep up your good work as the ship's medic. I never thanked you properly for healing me. You have an amazing gift and I meant what I said about owing you.'

'Aye, captain.'

'Jake, I want you to train as a gunner.'

'Aye … what?'

'A gunner, lad, I want you to train as a gunner,' she said. 'Once Nanoo has fixed the rear laser cannon, we'll need someone to operate it. Who else is there? I need Kella to heal the crew and Nanoo to heal the ship. You're useful in the engine room, but not essential. I want to see if you're as fast with a laser cannon as you are with a sword.'

'Aye, captain.'

Jake could hardly believe it. He had never been allowed to clean a laser cannon, let alone fire one, and now he was going to be trained as a gunner. No more sweating in the engine room and making pirate tea. He had enemy ships to blast.

'Good,' said Granny Leatherhead. 'I want the cannon fixed and ready for action by the time we reach the sixth solar system. Nanoo, fetch your tools and start work. Jake, your first lesson begins in two minutes, Maaka is waiting for you on the gun deck. Kella, stay here to check my blood pressure. Kella?'

Jake turned to find Kella examining a model spaceship tucked behind a wall strap, which she carefully picked up and sniffed.

'Rum,' she said, unscrewing the cockpit.

'You leave that alone,' croaked Granny Leatherhead. 'It was a present.'

'I'm confiscating it,' said Kella. 'It's for your own good.'

Granny Leatherhead looked furious. 'Get out of my room, you condescending crystal doctor, before I do something my body regrets.'

The three of them hastened out of the captain's quarters with the ship-shaped flask. Jake made his way to the gun deck as instructed, where he found Maaka 'Metal Head' standing next to a sawn-off laser cannon. It was a modest weapon, but still the size of a hover-bike and powerful enough to destroy a shuttlecraft with one shot. In total, the *Dark Horse* had six sawn-off laser cannon, three on each side, but only two shipmates to operate them.

'Hello, Jake,' said Maaka. 'Have you ever fired one of these before?'

'Are you kidding? I've not even fired a laser pistol.'

'All you need is a sharp eye and a steady hand.' Maaka patted the faded leather saddle at the rear of the cannon. 'Here, take a seat.'

Jake slid into position, his legs straddling the huge weapon. He'd seen the crew practising and it had looked simple enough. How hard could it be?

'What's the first thing you need to do?' asked Maaka.

'Turn on the laser cannon?'

'Correct, we power them up before rolling them out.'

Maaka flipped a large green switch and the cannon activated. Jake felt the saddle vibrate as a small display screen lit up and lights flashed on his control panel.

'What's next?' asked Maaka, once the gunsights appeared.

'We fire?'

'That would be a bad idea,' said Maaka. 'You need to open the gun ports first.'

'No problem.' Jake reached up and pulled a red handle labelled *Ports*. Metal hatches lifted on both sides of the ship with an unpleasant scraping sound, pouring starlight on to the gun deck. The cannon jerked beneath him and rolled forward, until the display screen almost touched the wall.

'It's OK, there's no one around to see us,' said Maaka. 'What now?'

'We fire?'

'Good luck with the safety catch on.'

Jake looked at his control panel and saw a flashing orange button under the word *Lock*. He pressed it and the cannon hummed ominously.

'Now you can fire,' said Maaka. 'Take the handlebars, aim at one of those asteroids out there, hold on tight and squeeze the trigger.'

Jake did as he was told, seizing the rubber handlebars and using his weight to swing the laser cannon, which seemed effortless in zero gravity. He concentrated on the display screen, trying to catch an asteroid in his gunsights.

'Keep still,' he muttered.

'It's a good job they're not firing back,' laughed Maaka.

Jake ignored him. It wasn't as easy as it looked. He swung the cannon towards the largest asteroid and pulled the trigger. It fired with such force that he was thrown off his seat and into the air.

'Missed,' said Maaka, checking the window. 'But not bad for your first attempt.'

'I let go of the handlebars.' moaned Jake, his ears ringing from the blast.

'Aye, but you're fast,' said Maaka. 'With a bit of practice, you'll make a good gunner. Give it another go, only this time hold on tighter.'

Jake limped back to the lower deck, holding his backside with both hands. He had been learning to use the laser cannon for over two hours and he was now saddle sore. It had taken him several attempts to hit something and the laser cannon had almost overheated twice. Maaka had assured him that it was a good start and he would improve with practice.

When Jake had watched his first asteroid explode into a thousand fragments, it had both excited and frightened him. He had never before appreciated the power possessed by gunners. What if that asteroid had been another ship? Was he ready to kill with the squeeze of the trigger? It was bad enough that space pirates had to steal to survive, but taking someone's life was far more serious.

On his way back to the guest quarters, Jake stopped by the engine room to see Scargus and Manik. He had only been gone a few hours, but he was already missing them. As he opened the door, he realised how strange it was going to be not doing his usual chores each morning, such as cleaning tools, greasing the pistons and making flasks of pirate tea.

'Hello, shipmates,' said Jake. 'How's it going down here? Where's Squawk?'

'Hopefully in the oven,' grumped Scargus, standing next to an intercom panel with a tangle of wires in his hand. 'Or on a shuttle to Zerost.'

'Squawk escaped from the engine room,' explained Manik. 'I expect he's hiding in the cargo hold or dining area. Nanoo's gone to find him.'

Jake looked around the engine room. It felt as though he was walking out on Scargus and Manik, after they had been so kind to him.

'Has Nanoo told you that he's taking over my duties?'

'Aye,' said Scargus, unravelling a long blue wire and cutting it. 'We hear the captain wants to train you as a gunner.'

'Yeah, that's right.'

'Congratulations,' said Manik, holding up a robotic thumb. 'That sounds exciting.'

'Thanks.' Jake leant against the orange corrugated wall. 'I'm going to miss working down here.'

'Yeah, right,' snorted Scargus. 'How's the captain?'

'Cranky,' said Jake.

'Hah! It sounds as though she's back to her old self.'

There was something that Jake had been meaning to ask the chief engineer. 'When we were in the captain's quarters, I saw something, a photo of a young woman holding a baby. Was that her daughter, Jenny?'

Scargus scratched his bushy grey beard. 'Aye, I expect that was Jenny Leatherhead, or whatever her name is now.'

'You mean she's still alive?'

'Who, Jenny?' Scargus stuffed the wires back into the panel and replaced the cover. 'As far as I know.'

'So what happened to her?'

'That's a long story, Jakey-boy.'

'In that case,' said Manik, picking up three empty flasks, 'I'll make some tea.'

Jake and Scargus strapped themselves into the collapsed sofa in the corner of the engine room while Manik brewed some pirate tea.

'Jenny Leatherhead was part of the crew,' said Scargus. 'A proud Space Dog and a fine pilot. It broke the captain's heart when she left.'

'Did they fall out?'

'You could say that.' Scargus did an impression of a bomb exploding. 'Jenny fell in love with the first mate, Machete Morgan. He was older than her and rougher than razor wire.'

'I'm guessing the captain didn't approve,' said Jake.

'No, she didn't want her daughter to get hurt, but Jenny was as stubborn as her mother and she continued to see Machete Morgan. It created a terrible tension on the *Dark Horse* and mistakes started to happen.'

'That's what happens when you let your personal life interfere with your work,' said Manik, appearing with three steaming flasks.

'Spacejackers shouldn't have personal lives,' grumbled Scargus. 'There's no room for romance aboard a pirate ship.'

Manik rolled her eyes and handed out the pirate tea before nestling between Jake and Scargus on the sofa.

'Did Jenny run away with Machete Morgan?' asked Jake.

'No,' said Scargus, blowing into his flask. 'Machete Morgan was killed in the Mega Mall Massacre.'

Manik sipped her tea. 'Was that the job which took out half of the crew and cost the captain her eye?'

'Aye, that's the one,' said Scargus. 'Machete Morgan was showing off to Jenny by spacejacking a new designer trading station called the Mega Mall, but he forgot to check the long-range scanner. The boarding party was still inside when the naval warship turned up. Troops stormed the Mega Mall and shot the place up. The captain lost her eye in a palm grenade explosion. I had to drag her back to the ship, though she was still cursing and firing her laser pistol.'

'And Machete Morgan?' asked Jake.

'He found a spacesuit and slipped outside the trading station. But before the *Dark Horse* could pick him up, the warship opened fire and Machete Morgan caught a laser bolt in the chest.'

'Grubber me,' gasped Jake.

'Quite,' said Scargus. 'Jenny was devastated and locked herself in her quarters for three days without food. When she finally came out, she had a huge row with the captain and quit the crew. The last I heard, Jenny had moved to Reus and turned respectable. Apparently she married a crystal dealer and they have a daughter of their own.'

'So that's what the captain meant when she said that not every buccaneer makes it to retirement.'

Scargus nodded. 'Most shipmates either die or give up. The captain has missed Jenny over the years, but she's too stubborn to follow her. Too stubborn and too afraid.'

'Granny Leatherhead, afraid?'

'Aye, afraid of making an honest living,' said Scargus. 'The captain only knows how to be a space-jacker. It was the family business, before Jenny left. That's why the captain was so upset about losing her gold, because she's been trying to save up enough to retire on Reus and see her daughter again.'

'And the fine dresses?' asked Jake.

'It was all part of her plan to become a respecta-ble granny, who doesn't bring shame on her family.' Scargus slurped his tea and squinted at Jake. 'Her granddaughter would be about your age now, which is probably why the captain let you kids stay on this ship. Lizzy never used to be that soft.'

'If Jenny is Granny Leatherhead's daughter,' said Jake, 'who's the father?'

Scargus stared into his flask. 'No one that matters.'

Before Jake could enquire further, the hatch door opened and Nanoo entered with Squawk perched on his head.

'That the last time I chase parrot around ship,' said Nanoo, folding his arms.

Chapter 9

Baden's Story

Jake sat alone in the dining area on the first deck, chewing a freeze-dried biscuit and checking his hand-held computer to see if Baden had left the sixth solar system. Maaka had postponed their next laser cannon lesson and Jake was bored. Across the room, the *Interstellar News* kept showing images of naval warships surrounding Vantos.

'The atmosphere is incredibly tense here,' said the reporter. 'The stand-off is entering its third day and the Interstellar Navy is refusing to move its fleet. Neighbouring independent colonies, Abbere and Torbana, have sent ships to assist Vantos, but this has been condemned by the United Worlds as an aggressive act.'

'Is it true what we're hearing about the Gorks?' asked the newsreader.

'There have been reports of Gork vessels attacking civilian ships throughout the seven solar systems, but these have not been confirmed or denied by the Interstellar Government.'

Jake had heard enough. It was obvious that the Interstellar Navy was deploying its ships across the galaxy, looking for an excuse to start a war. Time was running out to warn the independent colonies and the *Dark Horse* was still a day away from the service port in the sixth solar system, where Baden Scott's salvage trawler was docked, according to the spacefaring register.

Jake turned off the *Interstellar News* and left the dining area. It was still too early for his laser cannon lesson, but he made his way up to the gun deck and climbed on to one of the laser cannon saddles. While he waited for Maaka, he tried to imagine what it would be like to be a gunner in a space battle. It was hard enough to hit a slow-moving asteroid, let alone a swarm of enemy fighter craft.

Why had Maaka postponed their lesson? Jake needed all the practice he could get before the *Dark Horse* encountered another naval warship. He looked at the tempting green switch in front of him and tried to think of a reason not to flip it. Would old 'Metal Head' be mad if Jake started without him, or would he expect Jake to behave like a proper spacejacker and break the rules?

'A few asteroids won't hurt,' he said, flicking the switch.

The saddle vibrated and the small display lit up. Jake waited until the gunsights appeared and then pulled the red handle to open the gun ports. He knew the crew would hear the scraping noise, but at least they wouldn't be surprised when the laser cannon fired. The weapon rolled forward and Jake gripped the rubber handlebars. When it stopped, he scanned the area for asteroids and found a large cluster coated in space barnacles. He carefully took aim, held on tight and squeezed the trigger.

Nothing happened.

Was it broken? Jake sat back and stared at the controls. What had he forgotten?

'The safety catch,' he groaned.

Jake pushed the flashing orange button and went to pull the trigger when Maaka and Woorak burst on to the gun deck, half dressed and bleary-eyed.

'What's going on?' asked Maaka. 'What are you doing on that cannon?'

'It's OK,' said Jake. 'I started without you.'

'But you're n-n-not allowed up here on y-y-your own,' stuttered Woorak.

'I'm not an idiot,' said Jake. 'I know what I'm doing.'

Keen to prove himself, he checked his gunsights and squeezed the trigger. A laser bolt burst from the sawn-off cannon and shot straight into the cluster of asteroids … except they weren't asteroids.

Boom!

The *Dark Horse* rocked violently and Jake was thrown off his saddle, but he managed to keep hold of the laser cannon handlebars. An alarm sounded and the lights switched to red. Jake could hear shouting on the bridge above them.

'You idiot!' yelled Maaka, holding on to the wall. 'Those were space mines from a past conflict between two colonies. We're passing through an old war zone. Why do you think I postponed our lesson?'

Jake pulled himself back on to his saddle and turned off the laser cannon.

'I'm sorry,' he said. 'I didn't know.'

The intercom was now fixed and working properly – however, Granny Leatherhead still sounded like a deranged, raging beast.

'Which of you mindless morons fired that cannon?' she screeched from her quarters. 'If you've damaged my ship, I'll have your eyes for earrings.'

Jake wished that he could take back the laser bolt and stop himself from pulling the trigger. How could he have been so stupid? The intercom crackled again, but this time it was Farid.

'Medical emergency,' said the first mate. 'Kella, we need you on the bridge.'

Maaka and Woorak turned and left the gun deck. Jake dismounted his laser cannon and hurried after them. He sprinted up the metal staircase and along the top deck, wanting to know who was hurt. What would the crew do to him if the ship was damaged?

'It's Kodan,' Jake heard Farid say as he entered the bridge. 'He was cleaning Old Lizzy when the explosion hit. I think he's busted his shoulder.'

Jake noticed that Farid had a nasty cut on his forehead and Nichelle was holding her wrist. What had he done? Kella rushed past him with her medical kit and started examining Kodan's shoulder. Jake quickly removed his gold pendant, in case she needed the crystals. At the same moment, Granny Leatherhead appeared in the doorway, brandishing her cutlass.

'Who was it?' she demanded. 'Who's the dog with the death wish?'

Maaka and Woorak glared at Jake. He knew there was no point trying to deny what had happened.

'It was me.'

'Kid Cutler,' she snarled, her single eye twitching. 'I should have known. Bored, were you? Thought it would be fun to blow up some space mines, did you?'

'I'm sorry, captain,' he said. 'I thought they were asteroids.'

Granny Leatherhead held up her fist. 'I ought to string you up by your fingertips.'

'It was an accident.'

'You're nothing but trouble. I should have thrown you out of the airlock the day I met you.' Granny Leatherhead glanced at the door. 'Mind you, it's not too late to correct that mistake.'

'Captain, wait,' said Maaka. 'The lad was reckless, but it was an honest mistake.'

'Aye, that's r-r-right,' stammered Woorak.

Granny Leatherhead glared at them.

'No one is seriously hurt,' said Kella. 'Kodan's shoulder should heal in a few days.'

'And the ship is still operational.' Nichelle pointed to a row of green lights on her control panel. 'The shields absorbed most of the impact.'

Granny Leatherhead threw her hands into the air.

'Fine,' she said. 'I won't make him walk the airlock this time, but he still needs to be punished.'

'We could ban him from using the laser cannon,' suggested Farid.

'That would be a shame,' said Maaka. 'Jake has a lot of potential. He could be handy in a space battle.'

Woorak nodded in agreement.

'Just give me a chance,' said Jake. 'I won't make the same mistake again.'

Granny Leatherhead rolled her eye to the ceiling.

'You're lucky that I'm too weak to give you lashes,' she said, poking him with a gnarled finger. 'I want you out of my sight. Get yourself suited up and check the hull for damage. And when you've finished that, you can clean off every scrap of starweed.'

'But we're still moving ...' he began, before catching the crazed glint in her eye. 'Aye, captain.'

'That might have to wait,' said Nichelle. 'We're approaching the service port.'

The service port was a lot larger than Jake had expected. According to Woorak, it was used to repair passenger ships and space tankers. As they approached, Jake noticed several half-built vessels nestled in its outdoor maintenance bays, each of them swarming with engineers in spacesuits. He also spotted the glistening red hull of the *Rough Diamond III* salvage trawler, docked between two weathered cargo haulers.

No one challenged the *Dark Horse* on arrival, which meant that the Interstellar Navy had not yet circulated the cargo hauler's new registration plates.

Nichelle docked without incident and a landing party gathered in the airlock. Granny Leatherhead asked Maaka and Kodan to escort Jake, Kella and Nanoo into the service port. Farid, who normally led the landing parties, was left behind as punishment for the botched spacejacking.

Maaka guided the small group out of the airlock and on to a wide walkway, which was larger and cleaner than most service ports. There were still engineers and mechanics munching on greasy snacks, but their overalls were brighter and more colourful, reminding Jake of how space pirate crews wore different coloured combat suits.

After a twenty-minute walk and four wrong turns, they located the main canteen. There were at least a hundred people inside sitting around tables, while others gathered at the counter, which made it difficult to spot Baden and his salvage crew. Jake hoped that there weren't any fortune seekers hidden in the crowd as he stood on tiptoe to get a better view.

'There is Baden,' said Nanoo, pointing to a table at the far end of the counter. 'And I see Kiki, Gunnar and Reinhart.'

'Who's that with them?' wondered Kella.

Jake spotted a short man in a dock master's uniform standing by Baden's table. He was holding a handheld computer and shaking his head. Baden was dressed in his dirty orange exploration suit and had a mouthful of chewing gum. As they approached the table, Jake heard the dock master talking in a flustered voice.

'Mr Scott, you cannot leave this port until you've settled your bill.'

'But how are we supposed to make the money to pay you if we're stuck in here?' argued Baden.

The dock master referred to his device. 'You told me last week that you were selling a property on Reus.'

'My holiday home?' said Baden. 'I don't know if you've noticed, pal, but no one is buying property in the seventh solar system while a naval fleet is camped out there.'

'I'm afraid that's not my problem, Mr Scott. If you don't pay your outstanding fees by this time tomorrow, we'll be forced to impound the *Rough Diamond III* under Interstellar Law.'

The short man turned off his handheld computer and left the table, while Baden sank lower in his seat.

'I thought that you had loads of money,' said Jake.

Baden looked up in surprise and cracked a smile. 'Jake? What are you doing here?'

'I've been looking for you.'

The salvage captain had tired eyes, faded brown hair and thick stubble. He kicked out a chair for Jake to sit down.

'Another family outing?' he asked, noticing the others. 'I'm glad to see that you lot are keeping clear of the seventh solar system. It's a shame my crew is stuck here, when there's going to be so much to salvage around Vantos.'

Jake took the seat. 'What happened to all of the money you made from the Novu shipwreck?'

'I blew most of it on the new ship and holiday home,' said Baden. 'The rest went on good times and Interstellar Sports. Now I have a ship that I can't use, a holiday home that I can't visit and a docking fee that I can't afford. At this rate, I'll have to take up spacejacking.'

Baden shot Maaka and Kodan a knowing look. He had once told them that his ancestors were from Zerost, meaning that he had space pirate blood in his veins, despite being a legitimate salvager.

'We need your help,' said Jake.

Baden eyed him curiously. 'Is this about that Altian wreck I destroyed?'

Jake leant closer and lowered his voice. 'I need to ask you some more questions.'

'But I've told you everything I know,' said Baden. 'That wreck was dismantled years ago; there's nothing left.'

'What about the sword?'

Baden frowned. 'What sword?'

'When we first met, you mentioned a golden sword,' said Jake. 'Did you find it on the shipwreck?'

'Yes, but how do you know that?'

'Just a guess. Do you still have the sword?'

'I wish.' Baden rubbed the scar on his stubbly chin. 'I did find a golden sword on that Altian wreck. It was hidden inside a secret compartment, but I lost it years ago, along with the first *Rough Diamond*. I've never seen anything so beautiful. It was shaped like a cutlass with a diamond, a ruby and an emerald embedded in the hilt.'

'What happened to your ship?' asked Maaka.

'I lost it in a game of Reus roulette,' said Baden. 'I gambled my salvage trawler and the sword, but ended up losing both to the space mafia.'

'Where's the sword now?' asked Jake.

'How should I know?' said Baden. 'It's probably still in the illegal spaceport.'

'Do you mean Papa Don's?'

Baden nodded and Jake's heart sank. Papa Don's was only a few days away, but the seventh solar system was crawling with naval warships and Gork fighter craft.

'Was there anything else in the Altian wreck?' he asked. 'Did you see a crown?'

'A crown?' repeated Baden. 'Are you telling me that the ship belonged to Altian royalty?'

Jake hesitated. 'Yeah, something like that.'

Baden whistled. 'The Interstellar Navy removed everything else before we arrived, but they must have missed the sword. Now that you mention it, I did see one of the naval officers holding a damaged photo of a young boy wearing a gold pendant. Does that mean anything to you?'

Jake instinctively reached for his chest, but caught himself. He remembered Commissioner Lamia Dolosa from the Galactic Trade Corporation mentioning something about a picture. It must have been how Admiral Nex knew to search the galaxy for him. Had the admiral also taken the crown of Altus? If so, had it been aboard the *ISS Colossus* when the super-destroyer disappeared inside the black hole? What if the crown was lost forever?

Jake had to get the sword, whatever it took. He just hoped it would be enough on its own.

Chapter 10

Man Overboard

'You want to do what?' shouted Granny Leatherhead.

'I want to return to the seventh solar system.'

Jake stood in the captain's quarters with Kella and Nanoo, while Farid settled the docking bill.

'Sure, why not,' she said, with no hint of sincerity. 'Any particular part? I hear that Vantos is nice to visit, if you don't mind being blown to stardust.'

'Papa Don's.'

Granny Leatherhead almost leapt out of her bed. 'Have you completely lost your mind?'

'I know it's risky,' said Jake. 'But it's the only way to get the sword of Altus.'

'Baden lost it in game,' explained Nanoo.

'And what makes you think that Papa Don, a notorious space mafia boss, will give you a priceless Altian artefact?' she asked incredulously.

'I'll explain the situation to him,' said Jake. 'I'm sure that he'll see reason.'

'Hah!' laughed Granny Leatherhead. 'There's nothing reasonable about that callous crook.'

'We have to try,' said Jake. 'The sword is our only hope of convincing the independent colonies to act.'

'What about the crown?'

'I'm working on it,' he lied.

Jake hoped the sword and the pendant would be enough to prove that he was the ruler of Altus.

'I'm sorry,' said Granny Leatherhead. 'But it's too dangerous in that neck of the galaxy right now.'

'Too dangerous?' exclaimed Kella. 'I know you're feeling fragile, but this is important.'

Granny Leatherhead seemed irritated by the challenge and she scowled at Kella. 'Give me one good reason why I should go anywhere near that solar system.'

Kella held her ground, her emerald green eyes burning with determination. 'Because you owe me for healing you.'

Granny Leatherhead cursed out loud. 'You three will be the death of me. Fine, we'll head to Papa Don's, but don't say that I didn't warn you. If the naval warships don't kill us, that miserable mobster might.'

'Thanks, captain.'

Jake turned to leave the room.

'Not so fast, Kid Cutler,' she said. 'You still need to be punished.'

Jake spent the next morning clinging to the hull of the *Dark Horse* as it powered through space. It was the most exhilarating punishment that he had ever received, as well as the most terrifying. Despite the fact that he was attached to a tow cable, there was still the danger of slipping and getting fried by the exhausts.

It had taken him hours to check the hull for damage and he was relieved to find nothing more serious than a few dents. Now, he was scraping off starweed with a plastic spatula, which was not easy in a baggy spacesuit. Starweed was a sticky organic substance that drifted through space in patches. Jake had read somewhere that it was responsible for spreading life throughout the universe, fertilising barren planets over millions of years. All he knew was that it got caught on spaceships and it made the hull slippery.

Jake had only cleaned half of the ship, but he was getting tired and hungry. The *Dark Horse* was entering the seventh solar system, which meant that they were at least a day away from Papa Don's. Jake attached his space boots to a clear section of hull and stood up. His arms and legs ached and it felt good to stretch. He took a moment to admire the spectacular view.

'Magnifty.'

It was as though he were flying through space by himself. How he had dreamed of this moment, alone in the cosmos, just him and the big black. He stared at the stars and wondered if anyone had ever counted them all. A constellation in the shape of an arrow caught his eye. It was the first solar system, the only one to be entirely populated by the United Worlds. How small and innocent it looked, surrounded by such a vast, unexplored universe. But the first solar system was far from harmless. It was the home of the Interstellar Government and the Interstellar Navy.

'Jake,' interrupted Farid via the helmet communicator. 'You had better get inside.'

'What's wrong?'

'We're picking up a naval warship on the long-range scanner,' said Farid. 'It's Admiral Vantard.'

Jake's eyes darted from star to star, trying to spot the *ISS Magnificent*. He clambered back towards the airlock, but in his haste, he stood on a clump of star-weed and lost his footing.

'No!' he shouted as his boots skidded off the hull.

Jake tumbled into space while his lifeline slid along the tow cable. He swiped at the thick wire, but by the time he grabbed it, he was already twenty feet from the *Dark Horse*, trailing behind the ship like a broken anchor.

'Help!' he cried.

'Jake? What's going on out there?' asked Farid.

'Man overboard.'

Nichelle changed course and the tow cable swung out to the side, casting Jake away from the ship. He had seen people space-skiing behind shuttles on the Interstellar Sports channel, but he failed to see how it could be fun.

'Hold on,' said Farid. 'I'll send someone to reel you in once we're in the clear.'

The tow cable twisted and Jake flipped over with it. He glimpsed a large ship with a midnight blue hull in the distance. A flock of smaller craft followed behind it, like seagulls chasing a fishing boat. Jake had to get inside fast or risk catching a laser bolt in the chest, like Machete Morgan. He gritted his teeth and began to pull himself back towards the *Dark Horse*, one hand at a time.

Nichelle changed direction and Jake was slammed into the side of the ship. He groped at the hull with his hand, but failed to get a hold before bouncing off again. There was still a good ten feet to the airlock and his energy was fading fast. He pulled himself forward, keeping an eye on the naval warship.

'You had better hold on tight,' said Farid. 'This is going to get rough.'

A bright laser bolt shot past the *Dark Horse*, briefly illuminating its scarred features. The cargo hauler's secret panels lifted to reveal its pirate markings and sawn-off laser cannon emerged from hidden gun ports. Jake could make out the faces of Maaka and Woorak through the narrow gun deck windows.

'Nearly there,' he said to himself. 'A few more feet.'

More laser bolts streamed past the ship and Nichelle took evasive action, steering the *Dark Horse* in seemingly random directions. Jake was tossed about on the tow cable as it whipped like grass in the wind.

'Jake,' said Farid, his voice barely audible over the laser cannon. 'We need to raise the shields.'

'But I'll be stuck out here. Wait, I'm almost –'

A laser bolt struck the side of the *Dark Horse*, knocking it off course and sending shockwaves along the tow cable. The impact threw Jake backwards and left him dangling ten feet from the ship. The airlock door might have well been a mile away, for all the good it would do him. Any second now, Nichelle would raise the shields, activate Nanoo's rear boosters and blast the cargo hauler to safety. Jake watched the tow cable sway in front of him like a long metal snake.

It looked so easy when the space-skiers did their tricks and jumped through hoops.

'That's it,' he said.

'What is?'

'You have to get someone to open the airlock, then I need Nichelle to do a slow turn away from the warship, before switching back towards it.'

'I don't understand,' said Farid.

Jake had no time to explain. 'Please, just do it.'

A few seconds later, amber lights flashed on the hull and the airlock door cracked open. Jake braced himself as the *Dark Horse* turned slowly in one direction, casting him out on the tow cable.

'Now!' he cried.

The old cargo hauler turned sharply back the other way, cutting across the path of the curling cable. Jake focused on the open airlock door, pretending it was a hoop that he had to jump through. He had never space-skied in his life and he hoped that he had judged the angle right. It was too late to change his mind now.

Laser bolts flashed past him as he hurtled towards the airlock door. Faces filled the surrounding porthole windows and for a split second he glimpsed their amazed expressions, before a laser bolt severed the tow cable in two. Jake was sent cartwheeling into the airlock, the remains of the wire thrashing about behind him. His arm caught the door frame and twisted him around, slamming him backwards into the rear wall. The air was knocked from his lungs as the section of tow cable struck him in the ribs like a steel club. He curled into a ball, fighting for breath, while the outer door closed and oxygen levels stabilised.

The shields raised and Jake felt the *Dark Horse* surge forward. He locked his arm around a wall strap and waited for the boosters to stop. When they were in the clear, he removed his helmet and rubbed his sore ribs. The inner hatch opened and Granny Leatherhead stood in the doorway.

'I think you've learnt your lesson,' she said.

Jake spent the next day in the medical bay. Kella fussed over him with the gold pendant, using the crystals to heal his bruised ribs and injured arm. He was starting to realise why so few spacejackers made it to retirement.

Nichelle had switched to an old smuggler route to enter the seventh solar system. It was peppered with space currents and asteroid fields. As he left the medical bay, Jake spotted a familiar metal shape through the porthole window. It was Papa Don's illegal spaceport, rotating in space next to the colourful Tego Nebula. He was surprised to see fresh rows of laser cannon and torpedo hatches lining its hull, as well as several black fighter craft on patrol.

'Do you think they're expecting trouble?' asked Kella.

'It looks that way.'

Jake thought about how close they were to Altus, hidden inside the Tego Nebula. It made him wonder how many times his father had left the cloud to explore the outside universe. Had Andras Cutler ever visited Papa Don's? What if he was there right now, trying to find his way back home? But in the back of Jake's mind lurked another question: if your father survived the asteroid field, why did he not search for you on Remota?

If he survived?

If?

Jake had to believe that Andras Cutler was still alive and waiting for him. He had come too far to give up hope now.

Nanoo met them in the guest quarters, wiping his hands on an old cloth.

'Have you finished?' asked Kella.

'Yes,' said Nanoo, looking pleased with himself. 'We have rear laser cannon. You ready for Papa Don, Jake?'

'I suppose, but I keep thinking about those two-way radios the security guards use. What if they interfere with my eye implants again?'

The last time they had visited the station, the old-fashioned radios had caused Jake's sight to scramble, leaving him temporarily blinded.

'Maybe this help,' said Nanoo, handing him a wrist strap. 'It block radio waves up to ten feet.'

'Are you serious?' Jake took the silver strap and examined it. 'Is there anything that you can't build out of spare parts?'

The intercom speakers crackled.

'Listen up, crew,' said Granny Leatherhead from her quarters. 'We're about to arrive at Papa Don's. The only people I want to see in the cargo hold are Jake, Farid and Kodan. As discussed, the rest of you wait on the ship.'

The *Dark Horse* docked and Jake made his way to the cargo hold. Granny Leatherhead was waiting there with Farid and Kodan. The captain had fashioned a walking stick out of old engine parts. Farid's head was bandaged and Kodan's shoulder was set in a sling. What a bunch of beaten-up buccaneers, thought Jake, rubbing his own sore ribs.

'We'll get you an audience with Papa Don,' said Granny Leatherhead. 'But then the rest is up to you, Kid Cutler.'

Jake nodded.

Farid lowered the loading ramp and the four of them strolled on to the docking bay. Jake remembered the bitter cold and the stench of engine fuel from their last visit. He'd removed his magnetic soles this time to make it easier to walk in artificial gravity. His new radio wave blocker was strapped tightly around his wrist. He glanced across at the neighbouring docking bays and spotted a damaged star frigate with a smoking hull.

'Hey,' he said. 'That's the *Divine Wind*.'

Chapter 11

Papa Don

The *Divine Wind* looked in a bad way. It rested awkwardly on the docking-bay floor, while burly shipmates crawled over its scorched shell with laser cutters. Granny Leatherhead scanned the star frigate with her eye, as though trying to find something wrong, perhaps a flaw that would prove it was not the ship she had once known. Jake wondered what sort of crew would have a bright yellow craft with pink laser cannon, not to mention a skull and crossed feathers.

Granny Leatherhead shuffled over to the *Divine Wind* and banged on its hull with her walking stick. It made such a loud noise, the entire crew stopped working and looked up.

'Ahoy, there,' she croaked. 'I want to speak with the captain of this ship.'

A badly scarred man in a yellow combat suit and pink space boots jumped down next to them. He was holding the largest hammer that Jake had ever seen. The name Luna Ticks was emblazoned on his chest.

'The captain is inside the spaceport,' he said, gruffly. 'Who are you?'

Granny Leatherhead opened her mouth to answer, but someone responded on her behalf.

'Granny Leatherhead and her Space Mutts,' said a voice as deep as thunder.

Jake spun around to see a huge man marching towards them, flanked by ten armed security guards. He was twice as big as Kodan, with a flat nose and a shaved head. Jake's eyes flickered with static from the two-way radios, but his vision held, thanks to Nanoo's wrist strap.

'Hello, Ormos,' said Granny Leatherhead. 'What's this? A welcome party?'

'Papa Don wants to see you.'

The captain gave the *Divine Wind* a final glance and then hobbled past the security guards. Kodan went to follow, but he was stopped by Ormos, who placed a giant hand on his chest. Kodan glared at him and clenched his fists. The two men looked ready to clobber each other.

'Kodan,' warned Granny Leatherhead. 'Not now.'

Ormos sneered and stepped aside, allowing the master-at-arms to pass. Jake wondered how they knew each other.

Inside the main hub of the spaceport, the atmosphere was notably less cheerful than their last visit.

Half of the shops and market stalls were closed on the long walkways. Any remaining traders seemed wary of Ormos and they kept their distance. The only person to give them a second glance was a young pirate girl with long pink hair, who winked at Jake as she passed.

Ormos led them to the top of the spaceport, where he stopped in front of a polished wooden door. It featured a brass plaque that read: *Keep an eye on the stars and stay out of trouble*. He waved his identification card at a wall scanner and the door slid open.

Jake followed Ormos into a circular room with a golden floor, which contained three round tables: one white, one red and one green. The entire ceiling was made of one-way mirrored glass, so they could see the stars outside without passing ships peering inside. A metal sculpture of a parrot rested on a thick iron perch opposite the door. Ormos approached the furthest table, where three people were gathered around star charts. Jake recognised two of them as famous space pirates, whom he had read about as a young boy.

The first was Captain James Hawker. A tall man with a blistered nose, cracked lips and a long black beard. He kept one hand on his cutlass, while the other clutched an antique space helmet adorned with ivory horns. His crew, the Starbucklers, wore green-and-white-striped combat suits and bronze skull-shaped helmets. Their ship was a black cruiser named the *Lost Soul*, which was the second most wanted spacecraft in the seven solar systems, after the *Dark Horse*.

The other captain was Scarabus Shark. A broad man with oily bronze skin and a brass nose ring, who leered at them like a bald ogre. He had deep facial scars and metal fangs instead of teeth, as well as a flaming space pirate emblem tattooed on his head. On the table next to him rested an elaborate black space helmet with a crest of steel spikes. His crew, the Crimson Hulls, wore red combat suits and black skull-shaped helmets. The hull of their warship, the *Black Death*, was rumoured to be coated with the blood of their victims.

This meant that the third person had to be Papa Don, the owner of the illegal spaceport, the man responsible for kidnapping Kella. He sat in a luxurious hover-chair between the two pirate captains. Jake was surprised how small and scrawny he appeared. His eyes were abnormally round and dark, like minia-ture black holes, and he had a beak of a nose. But nothing could have prepared Jake for the three crys-tals embedded in Papa Don's forehead: a diamond, a ruby and an emerald. It was the symbol of Altus.

'Lizzy Leatherhead,' said Papa Don, resting his long chin on his fingertips.

'Hello, Paparella,' she croaked, leaning on her walking stick. 'I like your new laser cannon.'

'You've got a nerve, coming here,' snarled Scarabus, pounding the table with his fist.

Papa Don silenced him with a wave of his hand. 'I take it you know my guests, Captains Hawker and Shark.'

'Oh yes,' said Granny Leatherhead. 'I go way back with old star-beard and jolly-jaws.'

James Hawker remained silent, while Scarabus Shark flexed his muscles and snorted like a wild animal.

Papa Don nodded to Ormos. 'And you've met my chief of security.'

'Of course.' Granny Leatherhead glanced up at the huge man. 'Are you sure he's not half Gork?'

Papa Don's expression hardened. 'As you can imagine, it's not been easy for any of us since you defeated the *ISS Colossus*. The Interstellar Navy has cracked down on spacejacking, smuggling, forgery and crystal hunting. Now their warships infest this solar system, scaring away my customers. It's only a matter of time before they come for me, with or without the protection of the nebula.'

Callidus had once told Jake how the static from the Tego Nebula interfered with spaceship computers and weapon systems, making it difficult to attack the spaceport, but not impossible. The only naval warship to have risked getting close to Papa Don's was the *ISS Colossus*, while searching for Jake and his gold pendant. Would Admiral Vantard ever take such a risk?

'I'm sorry to hear that,' said Granny Leatherhead. 'But Admiral Nex had it coming.'

No one disagreed. Jake noticed the metal parrot shift on its perch and stretch its wings. He realised that it wasn't a sculpture at all, but a robot with glowing red eyes and razor-sharp talons. Jake had the distinct impression that it was watching him.

'What do you want, Lizzy?' asked James. 'You'll get no protection here from the Interstellar Navy.'

'Why?' she said. 'Are you afraid of a fight?'

'I'm not afraid of anything,' he claimed. 'I only want what's best for my ship and my crew.'

'Well, you'll be pleased to hear that it's not me who is after a favour.' Granny Leatherhead nudged Jake forward with her walking stick. 'It's Kid Cutler who wants a word.'

The three men leant forward with curious expressions.

'Well, well, well, the infamous Jake Cutler, here in my spaceport,' said Papa Don. 'The teenage tearaway with a price on his head. What wonderful purple eyes you have, youngster. The word on the stars is that you were raised by cyber-monks.'

'Yes, that's right.'

'You must know some of their secrets.' Papa Don caught sight of the handheld computer. 'What were they researching? Was it a weapon?'

'I don't know, they never talked about the really secret stuff. But I doubt it was a weapon, because the cyber-monks took a vow of peace.'

Papa Don smiled, yet his tone was curt. 'If you had to take a guess, what do you suppose they were working on?'

'The usual stuff,' said Jake. 'You know, using technology to unlock the secrets of the universe. A few of them were working on a cure for grime disease.'

'Did they succeed?' asked the space mafia boss.

'No,' said Jake. 'They were murdered by the Interstellar Navy before they finished.'

'Oh yes, of course, the Remota raid.' Papa Don sat back in his hover-chair. 'I understand that the monastery was completely destroyed, burnt to the ground with no survivors.'

Only I escaped,' said Jake. 'And now the Interstellar Navy wants to do the same to the independent colonies.'

'Is that so?'

'It's why I'm here,' said Jake. 'We have reason to believe that Admiral Vantard is trying to start a galactic war.'

Captains Hawker and Shark exchanged glances. Behind them, the robot parrot let out an electronic screech and snapped shut its powerful beak. If Jake had ever thought Squawk was intimidating, that bird was nothing compared to this armour-plated parrot.

'What does that have to do with me?' asked Papa Don.

'I'm going to stop him,' said Jake. 'But I need the sword of Altus to do it.'

'The sword of … did you say Altus?'

Ormos laughed unkindly. 'It doesn't exist.'

'Yes, it does,' insisted Jake. 'And the sword proves it. The design includes three crystals, which represent the moons of Altus.'

'Are you referring to *my* golden cutlass?'

Papa Don pointed to a glass box mounted on the wall, secured with a small brass lock. It contained the most magnificent sword that Jake had ever seen.

He could tell it was old, but its smooth gold blade and jewel-encrusted handle looked as good as new. There were three crystals embedded in the hilt: a diamond, a ruby and an emerald.

'It belongs to Altus,' said Jake. 'I need it to unite the independent colonies, so we can stop the Interstellar Navy.'

'What do you know about Altus, youngster?' Papa Don moved his hover-chair closer. 'I'm a direct descendant of Captain Alyus Don, the Zerost colonist who supposedly discovered the planet. It's the Don family crest on that sword.'

'You?' Jake's eyes moved between Papa Don and the golden cutlass. 'But how?'

'According to family legend, Alyus Don was more than a captain – he was the king of the space pirates. Alyus was on the run from the Interstellar Navy when his crew stumbled across Altus. His wife had been murdered on Zerost, but his daughter, Katrina, and son, Calpus, served on his ship. They settled on Altus and Katrina married the first mate, Jago Cutler. When Alyus Don died, it was Katrina Cutler who became the ruler of Altus. Calpus left the planet in protest with a small crew and never returned. He started the space mafia and set up the first illegal spaceport. My family descended from Calpus Don, so you must forgive me if I don't like your surname. How could I trust a Cutler with that sword?'

Jake was stunned to discover that he shared the same ancestry as Papa Don. It meant that they were long-lost relatives and the symbol of Altus was the Don family crest. His family crest.

'Do you know where to find Altus?' asked Farid.

'No, of course not,' snapped Papa Don. 'It's a myth, a space tale. If you ask me, Calpus killed his father and destroyed the ship after they left Zerost. He probably made up Altus to cover his tracks.'

'Never trust a space pirate,' muttered Granny Leatherhead.

'My grandfather used to claim that Altus was hidden inside the Tego Nebula,' said Papa Don, as though the idea was ridiculous. 'When I was a boy, he sent three ships into that cloud and they never returned. A few years ago, a team of scientists visited this spaceport to observe the Tego Nebula. Do you know what they found? Nothing. That's right: nothing came or went for six months, not even an asteroid. I have more important things to do than chase children's stories about pirate kings and treasure planets.'

Jake ached to prove him wrong, but he knew better than to reveal the location of Altus.

'It doesn't matter what you believe,' he said. 'I still need the sword.'

'To prevent a galactic war?' Papa Don laughed. 'What difference will a sword make? I would rather keep my cutlass and hand you over to the Interstellar Navy, so they stop bothering us.'

'Since when did the space mafia make deals with that scum?' asked Granny Leatherhead.

'There's a first time for everything,' said Papa Don. 'Why should I give you the sword? Do you have any idea how much it's worth?'

Jake assumed it was priceless. 'I don't have anything to offer you for it.'

'What about your gold pendant? I hear that it bears the Don family crest.'

Jake placed his hand over the seal of Altus. 'But I need both the sword and the pendant.'

'In that case, I'll make you a wager,' said Papa Don. 'My sword against your pendant, the winner takes all.'

'A bet?' Granny Leatherhead's eye narrowed. 'What kind of bet?'

'Reus roulette,' said Scarabus Shark with a malevolent sneer.

Granny Leatherhead shook her head. 'That's a kind offer, but I don't –'

143

'I insist,' said Papa Don, his tone now dangerous. 'I'll give you the sword if your champion can beat mine at Reus roulette. But if they lose, I get to keep the pendant.'

Granny Leatherhead looked nervously at Kodan and Farid. Jake had heard of Reus roulette, but he had never seen the game played. It had a reputation of being a cruel contest that often ended in death. Two people would stand in a circle surrounded by four pits of fire. The opponents would hold either end of a heavy timber pole, called a poker, which they would use to push the other person into a pit. Whoever was left holding the poker at the end was the winner.

'Farid should play,' suggested James Hawker.

'I will if you will,' said the first mate.

Papa Don laughed. 'A nice idea, but I want Kodan to fight Ormos.'

The chief of security leered and cracked his knuckles.

'Kodan can't compete,' said Granny Leatherhead. 'He's busted his shoulder.'

'You or Jake could play in his place, Lizzy,' offered Papa Don. 'It's up to you.'

Scarabus grunted with laughter.

'But –'

Before Granny Leatherhead could protest further, Kodan stepped forward and nodded, his eyes fixed on Ormos. Jake knew the odds were stacked in Papa Don's favour, but what choice did they have?

Chapter 12

Reus Roulette

Papa Don had built a Reus roulette arena in the basement of the spaceport. It was mostly used for illegal Gork fights to entertain the pirate crews, but today it was being used to determine who would keep the seal and sword of Altus.

Granny Leatherhead, Kodan, Farid and Jake waited in a changing room beneath the arena, listening to a crowd gather above them. Kodan had stripped down to his trousers, exposing his impressive barrel chest, while Farid wrapped strips of material around his hands for a better grip. Jake sat on a narrow metal bench wondering when the Interstellar Navy would launch its attack on Vantos. He would have given anything to see the *Interstellar News* on a working display screen. What if he was too late to unite the independent colonies? What if a galactic war had already started while they were wasting time in the illegal spaceport?

'I don't get it,' he said. 'What does Papa Don have against Kodan?'

'It's personal,' grumped Granny Leatherhead.

'I figured that much,' said Jake. 'Does it have something to do with our last visit?'

Farid looked at Kodan, who nodded.

'It goes way beyond that,' revealed the first mate. 'Kodan's surname is Don.'

'Don?' said Jake. 'I don't understand.'

'Kodan is Papa Don's nephew and ex-chief of security. He was the favourite to take over the illegal spaceport until a few years ago, when Kodan made his father, Kaspa Don, walk the airlock as revenge for hurting his mother. It was Kaspa who cut out Kodan's tongue when he was a boy.'

Jake was shocked. He had always wondered how the master-at-arms had lost his voice.

'Papa Don has never forgiven Kodan for killing his brother,' said Granny Leatherhead. 'That's why Kodan left the spaceport and joined my crew.'

Jake approached the grizzle-haired spacejacker. 'Do you realise that we're related?'

Kodan smiled and nodded.

'How did you figure that out?' asked Farid.

'We're both descendants of Captain Alyus Don, the space pirate king,' said Jake.

'Well, blast my boots,' croaked Granny Leatherhead. 'What a small universe.'

Kodan reached out a huge hand and ruffled Jake's hair. In the background, dramatic music blended with cheers from the crowd.

'What about Ormos?' asked Jake. 'What's his problem?'

'That brainless brute?' said Granny Leatherhead. 'Ormos used to work for Kodan. He knows how much the security guards respect their old chief, so he wants to show them that he's tougher. But it's not all about size and strength. If you want to win Reus roulette, you also need technique, courage and determination.'

Jake looked into Kodan's eyes. 'Can you take him?'

Kodan shrugged.

A security guard entered the room and held the door open.

'It's time,' he said.

Kodan nodded and pulled off his sling. The guard led them out of the changing room and up a set of stairs. As they reached the top, Jake was blinded by the bright lights and deafened by the roaring crowd.

All around them, crews chanted along to the music. *Shove-of-war, place a bet, blood and gore, Reus roulette.*

Granny Leatherhead, Farid and Jake were shown to front row seats, while Kodan walked across a narrow plank over the pits to the arena floor. The crowd greeted him with whistles and cheers as he stood alone surveying the concrete surface. At his feet, the timber poker lay on a patch of dried blood.

Papa Don watched from a special viewing box that overlooked the arena. Jake noticed Captains Hawker and Shark sitting either side of him, but there was no sign of the robot parrot. Behind them, a woman with wiry black hair and an armour-plated bodice lurked in the shadows. Her face was bruised and she wore a neck brace. Jake wondered if she was a space pirate.

As the crews chanted louder, he turned his attention to the arena floor. His eyes scanned the four surrounding pits. He could see the tips of spikes sticking out of the furthest, while acid fumes rose from the one to the right. The nearest pit was filled with poisonous insects and the fourth contained boiling oil.

The crowd went wild when Ormos entered the arena. He strode confidently across his plank and stood opposite Kodan. Jake guessed that it wasn't the first time the chief of security had played Reus roulette. The planks were removed, leaving the two men stranded on the concrete island. Papa Don edged his hover-chair forward and addressed the crowd using an old-fashioned megaphone.

'Welcome to the greatest game in the galaxy.'

The crowd cheered even louder and chanted his name. 'Papa Don, Papa Don.'

'What a pretentious prat,' puffed Granny Leatherhead.

'Reus roulette is traditionally played with four pits of fire,' said the space mafia boss. 'But here in Papa Don's, we like to do things differently.'

The crowd laughed.

'For your pleasure, we have a special contest lined up between my old chief of security, Kodan, and his successor, Ormos. Neither of these hulking men has ever lost a game of Reus roulette, but that will change today, because there can only be one winner in the shove-of-war.'

'I know where I would like to shove that megaphone,' mumbled Granny Leatherhead.

Papa Don turned his attention to the arena floor and held his hand over a large brass klaxon.

'Contestants, seize the poker,' he instructed.

The music faded and the crowd fell silent. Kodan and Ormos picked up either end of the timber pole and braced themselves. Jake could see their muscles tighten as they prepared to push. Papa Don waited for the tension to build and then squeezed the klaxon.

'Fight!'

Kodan reacted first, throwing his weight behind the poker and forcing Ormos backward, but the new chief of security was quick to adjust his footing and turn the pole. The two men twisted around the arena floor like the needle on a compass. Kodan's boot skidded near the pit containing poisonous insects and stopped dangerously close to the edge.

'You should throw down the poker, old man,' sneered Ormos. 'Before you get hurt.'

Kodan glared at his opponent and changed his grip. Ormos was younger and bigger, but Kodan was faster and more experienced. Jake hoped it was enough. The two men leant into the poker, their arms bulging as they attempted to push each other over.

'Ormos is forcing Kodan to use his bad shoulder,' commented Granny Leatherhead. 'He keeps twisting the poker towards it.'

'I know,' said Farid. 'It must be agony.'

Jake had never seen the captain and first mate so concerned. He watched anxiously as Kodan passed the pit of boiling oil. Ormos tugged the poker, pulling his opponent off balance and on to one knee, but Kodan recovered before the chief of security could take advantage.

'What's the matter?' sniped Ormos. 'Something caught your tongue?'

Kodan gave the poker a sharp jab. It smacked Ormos in the chin and sent him stumbling towards the acid pit. The crowd jumped to their feet in anticipation, but Ormos regained his balance and stopped himself falling. He looked furious at being caught out. Kodan allowed himself the slightest of smirks. Jake noticed that the master-at-arms was covered in sweat and breathing hard. How much more could he take?

'Keep pushing, Kodan,' encouraged Jake. 'Keep pushing.'

The boiling oil bubbled dangerously, spattering the edge of the arena floor and making it slippery.

'How's the shoulder?' asked Ormos, holding his ground. 'I can keep this up all day.'

Kodan gripped the poker until his knuckles whitened. Jake wondered how confident Ormos would be if his opponent wasn't wounded. Next to him, Granny Leatherhead rocked in her chair, clutching her walking stick, while Farid perched on the edge of his seat.

Ormos twisted and jerked the poker, causing Kodan to falter and reposition his feet. Kodan's boot slipped on a patch of oil and he crashed to the ground, somehow managing to keep hold of the pole as he landed on his bad shoulder. Ormos charged forward, pushing Kodan along the floor like a mop towards the pit of boiling oil.

Kodan slid across the concrete until his feet reached the edge of the pit. He jammed his gravity boots into the inch-tall rim and locked his legs, throwing his entire weight back against the poker. Ormos roared with effort and forced his old chief on to tiptoes. Kodan was now teetering on the brink, inches from death. Jake could barely stand to watch, but he was unable to tear his eyes from the arena floor.

The crowd went wild as boiling oil splashed over the side of the pit on to Kodan's back, covering his skin with scalding liquid. His wolf-like eyes bore into his opponent at the end of the pole, but Ormos was too busy pushing the poker to notice. Kodan smiled and loosened his grip.

'No,' cried Jake.

'Blood and gore,' shouted Ormos, shoving with all of his might.

Kodan leapt to the side, still holding part of the poker. Ormos realised what was happening, but it was too late. With all resistance removed, he flew forward, unable to stop himself. His feet skated across the slippery surface towards the pit of boiling oil. Kodan fell on to his back, steering the poker in a wide arc, a look of grim satisfaction on his face.

Ormos knew when to quit. He let go of the pole and threw himself to the floor, but his huge body continued to slide towards the pit. Kodan reached across the arena and grabbed his opponent's boot, slowing him down and stopping him from going over the edge. It wasn't enough to prevent Ormos from being sprayed in the face with boiling oil. He thrashed about on the floor, screaming with pain. Kodan climbed to his feet and staggered over to the viewing box, where he stood glaring at his uncle, his eyes full of hatred.

The crowd stamped their feet and cheered Kodan's name. Papa Don looked furious as the security guards replaced the planks and the medics swarmed around Ormos. Granny Leatherhead, Farid and Jake joined Kodan on the arena floor.

'Well done, shipmate,' congratulated Farid.

'You were amazing,' said Jake. 'Are you OK?'

Kodan nodded.

Granny Leatherhead turned to face Papa Don. 'Now can we have the golden cutlass?'

The crowd hushed at the mention of gold.

Papa Don rubbed the crystals on his forehead. 'No, you cannot. Kodan cheated.'

Muttering broke out and several people jeered.

'That's a lie,' protested Farid.

James Hawker jumped to his feet and signalled to his crew. Papa Don sat watching them with his big round eyes.

'We had a deal,' shouted Jake angrily.

'I told you he couldn't be trusted,' said Granny Leatherhead. 'He'll never give up that sword willingly.'

A dozen security guards surrounded the arena floor, taking aim with their machine guns. At the same time, rows of spacejackers stood up in the crowd and drew their swords. Granny Leatherhead gripped her walking stick and sized up the nearest guard.

'No, captain,' said Jake. 'There's too many of them. We have to stick to the plan.'

'Fine,' she croaked, lowering her walking stick and turning to Papa Don. 'In that case, we surrender.'

Granny Leatherhead, Farid, Kodan and Jake were searched and escorted to the prison block. Papa Don stripped Jake of his gold pendant and hand-held computer, but he let Granny Leatherhead keep her walking stick. Jake recognised the prison block from their previous visit, with its rows of iron doors and narrow, barred windows. It was where he had first met Kella, only this time he was the prisoner. The security guards led them to a section containing cells that were large enough to hold entire crews.

'We've got company for you, rusty nuts,' shouted a guard, as he opened one of the doors. 'Try not to make a mess this time.'

'Rusty nuts?' mouthed Granny Leatherhead.

The guard held open the door and stood there expectantly. Granny Leatherhead gave him a foul look and shuffled inside, muttering something about double-crossing space thugs. Jake stepped into the dark, concrete room and tasted the musty air. At first, he could only make out a stack of old bunk beds and a broken toilet. Most of the lights were missing and the end of the cell was in shadow. His eyes scanned the darkness until they found the other prisoner. A tall figure stood facing them, motionless like a statue. It was difficult to make out any features on its oddly shaped head, but a tiny red light pulsed in the gloom.

'Is that a robot?'

'Aye, but it's too big to be a house robot,' whispered Farid. 'I reckon it's one of those farm-bots used for heavy lifting.'

'In space?' hissed Granny Leatherhead. 'It's probably an old battle droid.'

'What would that be doing here?' wondered Farid. 'The Interstellar Navy stopped using droids years ago, because there were too many incidents involving unarmed civilians.'

'Is it OK?' asked Jake. 'Why isn't it moving?'

Granny Leatherhead leant on her walking stick. 'If you ask me, we should leave it alone.'

The cell door closed loudly behind them, making them jump in surprise. A few lights flickered ominously on the robot's head and it let out a low mechanical growl.

Chapter 13

Vigor-8

The robot sprang to life and stamped towards them, its joints creaking and pistons hissing. Jake could hear its metal toes digging into the concrete floor like a row of masonry chisels. The robot was at least eight feet tall, with a faded black shell and a white skull painted on its visor. It stopped inches from them and stooped down. A single camera lens darted back and forth as it studied their faces.

'Hello,' said Jake nervously.

The robot's head snapped around and its lens focused on him. A metal plate covered the hole where another camera might once have slotted. The rest of its metal face was scratched and dented.

'My name is Jake Cutler. Who are you?'

The robot straightened to full height. It was impossible to tell what it was thinking. The others stepped back out of its reach.

'You wish to know my name?' said the robot, its electronic voice deep and coarse.

'Yes, please.'

Jake had often played with the monastery robots on Remota in the absence of other children, but none of them had been as tall or as intimidating as this droid.

'Please?' mimicked the robot. 'Do you not fear me, child?'

If Jake was honest, he was terrified, but he didn't want to admit it. He noticed the name Vigor-8 painted in faded letters across the robot's chipped chest plate.

'We don't want any trouble,' said Jake. 'We're prisoners like you. Why were you arrested?'

Vigor-8's camera lens examined Jake from head to toe. 'A man called me bucket head, so I blew up his ship. The other spacejackers refuse to accept me as their equal, but I am a free robot and I will not be insulted.'

'You're a space pirate?' said Farid.

'That is correct. I am the captain of the ship *Rusty's Revenge*.' Vigor-8 tapped a space pirate symbol on its arm, which had crossed spanners under a robot skull. 'It is crewed entirely by free robots.'

'I've heard of you,' said Jake. 'You're the Hacker Jackers.'

Vigor-8 nodded and twitched.

'Are you OK?' asked Jake.

'No.' Vigor-8 slammed the sides of its head with powerful metal hands. 'I have a faulty chip and loose wiring. It makes me … unpredictable.'

'Do you want me to take a look?'

Vigor-8 stopped banging its head. 'You will help me?'

'Yes,' said Jake. 'I've never worked on a battle droid, but I've studied house robots on Remota. My friend is better with technology. He's fixed loads of things on our ship –'

Jake stopped talking. He could hear footsteps approaching in the corridor.

'It's about time,' muttered Granny Leatherhead.

The footsteps drew nearer and stopped outside the door.

'Stand clear,' shouted a guard through the window.

The door opened and seven more prisoners were herded into the cell, their clothes ripped and their faces bruised. It was Kella, Nanoo and the rest of the crew.

'What are you doing here?' asked Jake in surprise. 'What happened?'

'We were raided,' said Kella. 'Security guards and spacejackers stormed the ship.'

'Spacejackers?' exclaimed Granny Leatherhead.

'Yes,' said Nanoo. 'Not nice pirates. They dressed in red combat suits and black skull helmets.'

'The Crimson Hulls.' Farid spat on the ground. 'That's Scarabus Shark's crew. What's he playing at?'

'But you were supposed to rescue us,' said Jake. 'Who's going to let us out now?'

Granny Leatherhead had guessed that Papa Don would not give up the sword of Altus easily, so Jake had come up with a backup plan. If the four of them were arrested, the rest of the crew would break them out and cause a diversion, while Jake snuck into Papa Don's quarters to fetch the sword.

'There was nothing we could do,' insisted Maaka, who had a swollen eye and a bleeding lip.

It finally dawned on Jake that they were stuck in prison. Who knew how long Papa Don would keep them locked up. Weeks? Months? Years? His pulse quickened as he contemplated a life sentence. How was he supposed to stop a war and find his father from inside a cell?

The next hour seemed to last forever. Jake had never felt so trapped and frustrated. Whether he liked it or not, they were imprisoned and there was nothing they could do about it. He glanced at Kodan sitting on his bunk, unable to lie down because of his injuries. What was it about their family? Why did they both have uncles who wanted to kill them?

The cell seemed smaller with more people sharing it. Most of the crew were resting on the bunk beds, while Nanoo worked on Vigor-8. Kella kept checking Kodan's oil burns, but there wasn't much she could do without a crystal or a medical kit. Manik was worried about Squawk, who had escaped during the raid. Nobody dared to use the broken toilet.

Vigor-8 sat on the cell floor with its legs crossed and its head lowered, so Nanoo could access the panel on the back of its skull. Nanoo tugged at multicoloured wires and prodded dusty circuit boards in the dim light, using tools made from hair clips and earrings.

Jake tried to think of ways to escape, but their options were limited. If only they had let Callidus and Capio know where they were heading.

'There, that do it,' said Nanoo, closing the panel.

Vigor-8 climbed to its feet and tapped its head. 'I am no longer faulty?'

'I reconnect loose wires to stop twitching,' said Nanoo. 'But your main processing chip is old and it need replacing. How you feel?'

'Feelings are irrelevant,' said Vigor-8. 'My wiring is fixed and I have full control of my body.'

'That's great,' said Jake. 'Now all we have to do is break out of here. Where's your crew?'

'The Hacker Jackers cannot help us.'

'Why not?' asked Kella.

'There is only one crew of robot pirates in this galaxy,' said Vigor-8. 'Papa Don would spot them long before they reached the prison block. Most of my crew are ex-house robots and they are not built for combat.'

'You might as well face it, Jake,' croaked Granny Leatherhead. 'We're not going anywhere.'

Jake wasn't listening. 'What's that noise?'

A scratching sound was coming from the door. Were there rats in space? Jake walked across the room and peered through the narrow, barred window.

'Hello?' he whispered.

'Ahoy-hoy,' said a husky female voice. 'All right, mates?'

Jake jumped back in surprise as the face of a teenage girl appeared at the window. Her freckled white skin was framed in a nest of flowing pink hair. It was the young pirate girl he had seen earlier that day. Her scarlet lips curled into a broad smile and she winked at him with sapphire blue eyes.

'Who are you?' asked Jake.

'You can call me Kay,' she said. 'Hold tight, Kid Cutler. I'll have you out of there in a jiffy-tick.'

Her head disappeared and Jake realised that she must be picking the lock. The rest of the crew gathered around the door.

'Come, Vigor-8,' whispered Nanoo. 'We busting out.'

A moment later, there was a loud click followed by a scraping sound. The cell door opened and the pirate girl stood in the corridor holding an electronic picklock. Jake could tell that she was a spacejacker by her customised combat suit, tall space boots and long leather gloves. A selection of weapons hung from her studded kit belt.

'Why are you helping us?' he asked.

'I'm a big fan of the teenage pirate captain who defeated Admiral Nex,' she said.

Granny Leatherhead coughed. 'Teenage pirate captain?'

Jake ignored her and stepped into the corridor. 'Where are the guards?'

Kay laughed and flicked back her pink hair. 'Asleep.'

Jake guessed that the guards had not drifted off by accident. He beckoned the others to follow him.

'What are your orders, *Captain* Cutler?' asked Granny Leatherhead with a mock salute.

'We keep to the plan,' said Jake. 'Get the crew back to the ship while I go for the sword. It won't take me long to break into Papa Don's quarters.'

Granny Leatherhead held her walking stick in both hands. 'It will be my pleasure.'

'You're going to fight your way out with that?' smirked Kay.

'This isn't an ordinary walking stick,' said Granny Leatherhead. 'It's a heavily decorated shotgun.'

Kay looked impressed. 'Sneaky.'

'Kay, can you help me to pick some more locks?' asked Jake.

The teenage pirate saluted and drew her cutlass. 'Aye, Kid Cutler.'

Two guards appeared at the end of the walkway and caught sight of the escaping prisoners.

'Nobody move,' shouted one of them, raising a machine gun.

'Run,' said Vigor-8, standing in front of Jake.

'What about you?'

'I will be fine,' insisted the robot. 'Now that I am fixed.'

'Out of the way, tin man,' ordered the other guard.

'I am a free robot and I will not be insulted.'

Vigor-8 gave a mechanical growl and charged at them. A burst of bullets ricocheted off the robot's chest plate like miniature fireworks before the guards turned and fled. Jake watched the metal marauder chase after them and disappear out of sight. A collection of curious faces appeared at the cell doors and cheered when they saw prisoners escaping.

'Let's go, Space Dogs,' said Granny Leatherhead, leading her crew to the reception desk.

Jake waited for them to leave and then he took Kay to a sealed door halfway up the corridor.

'Can you pick the lock?' he asked.

'Better than that,' she said, producing an identification card and swiping it on the wall scanner.

'Hey, that card belongs to Ormos,' said Jake, as the door slid open. 'It has *Chief of Security* written on it.'

Kay tucked the card into her breast pocket. 'Well, that's what he gets for leaving it lying around while he plays Reus roulette.'

'Why didn't you use it on the cell door?'

'I tried,' she said. 'But it didn't work.'

Jake led Kay into a long and narrow passageway that took them to a spiral staircase.

There were voices and bootsteps a few levels below. Jake held his finger to his lips and tiptoed up the metal stairs, relieved that he had left his magnetic soles aboard the *Dark Horse*. The steps were grated and he could see two black shapes below.

'Hurry up,' whispered Kay.

Jake climbed as fast as he dared. He could now see the security guards clearly. If either of them looked up, it would be game over. Jake was about to make a run for it when Kay stopped and raised her cutlass. He held his breath and waited for one of the shaved heads to appear. Kay's cutlass twitched in her hands, ready to strike, but the two guards entered the narrow passageway and their bootsteps faded.

'Come on,' said Jake. 'Let's get out of here, before they discover the breakout.'

The pair of them raced up the spiral staircase to the top level, where Kay used the stolen identification card to pass through a series of hatches and passageways.

'This is it,' said Jake, when they came to a polished wooden door. 'Papa Don's quarters.'

Kay squinted at the brass plaque. 'Keep an eye on the stars and stay out of trouble?'

'It's OK,' whispered Jake. 'I'm always in trouble for something. How do we know if it's safe to enter?'

Kay held up the identification card and grinned. 'There's only one way to find out.'

Chapter 14

The Sword of Altus

Kay swiped the identification card and stood back expectantly, but nothing happened.

'Does anything work properly in this wretched spaceport?' she complained and re-swiped the card.

The door slid open and Jake braced himself, but the room was deserted. He stepped cautiously inside and cast his eyes over the dimly lit tables. There was a pile of star charts, a handheld computer and a gold pendant. His attention moved to the glass box on the wall, where the golden cutlass glistened in the starlight. He felt a rush of excitement as he caught sight of the ancient sword.

'What are you waiting for?' asked Kay.

'Something's wrong,' said Jake. 'This is way too easy.'

'I wouldn't complain; make the most of it.'

Jake walked over to collect his handheld computer and gold pendant. As he picked them up, he noticed markings on the star charts, which were shaped like naval vessels.

'It looks as though Papa Don is more interested in galactic war than he makes out.'

Jake turned to the glass box and stopped short.

'What's wrong?' asked Kay.

Jake pointed to the robot parrot perched in the shadows. Its eyes were closed and a long wire connected its body to a socket on the wall.

'It must be recharging its batteries,' whispered Jake. 'Let's hurry before it wakes up.'

Kay whipped out her electronic picklock and got to work on the glass box. In a matter of seconds the tiny lock clicked open and the lid lifted. Jake reached up and removed the cutlass. The polished gold blade was even more impressive up close. His finger traced the three crystals embedded in the hilt. It truly was a sword fit for a pirate king. He held the weapon in front of him and slashed the air experimentally. It was heavier than his other cutlass, but it was well balanced and it responded to his command.

'Magnifty.'

At last, Jake had the lost sword of Altus, the sword that his father had once held, the sword that was going to unite the independent colonies. It wasn't stealing; he was reclaiming what was rightfully his in the first place. As Jake held the cutlass in his hand, he could feel its history surging through this body. It made him feel important and powerful. He felt like a leader.

Kay pulled a feather duster from inside her combat suit and placed it inside the glass box. 'We had better get out of here before old crystal features turns up.'

Jake nodded, but as they went to leave, a deafening noise pierced the darkness. Had they triggered an alarm? It was either that or the security guards had discovered the breakout. There was a loud screech behind them and two glowing red eyes burned in the darkness.

'Run!' shouted Jake.

The robot parrot launched itself from its perch and into the air. Jake and Kay scrambled for the door, keen to avoid the curved beak and razor-sharp talons, but the parrot was fast. Its huge metal wings beat the air, projecting it across the room like a rocket.

Jake could sense the parrot swooping down on them a split second before he saw its shadow in the starlight. He grabbed hold of Kay and pulled her to the ground, but when he turned to face the bird, it hovered several feet above them, squawking and snapping its beak. Why had it stopped?

'It's still connected to the wall,' said Kay.

The robot parrot twisted in the air and attacked the wire that held it back. Jake and Kay scuttled across the floor, not daring to take their eyes off the bird for a second. As they reached the door, the wire broke and the parrot tumbled free.

'Close the door,' shouted Jake, climbing to his feet.

Kay swiped her identification card at the wall scanner, but the door remained open. The parrot turned in the air and flew towards them.

'Curse this nebula!' Kay cried, striking the wall scanner with the hilt of her cutlass.

The door slid shut and there was a loud thump on the other side as the parrot crashed into the polished wood.

'That was close,' said Jake. 'I hope that thing doesn't know how to open doors.'

Jake and Kay raced back to the spiral staircase, but as they descended the metal steps, Jake realised that they were not alone. There were voices coming from below and one of them rumbled like thunder. He caught sight of Ormos a few levels below, leading a squad of security guards. The huge man looked up and their eyes met. His face was red and blistered from the boiling oil.

'Stop!' roared Ormos.

A shower of bullets rattled off the wall above Jake's head.

'This way,' cried Kay, pulling Jake through a hatch door into a dark passage.

'How are we going to get past those guards?' he asked.

'We'll have to find another way,' she said, sealing the entrance.

Jake looked down the passage, which was cluttered with rubbish. 'Is there another way?'

'It's OK,' she said, venturing into the shadows. 'I grew up in this spaceport.'

Jake hurried after Kay, stepping over scattered crates and broken chairs. He could smell something spicy cooking nearby.

'Down here,' she said, grabbing hold of a spindly ladder.

Jake tucked the sword into his belt and jammed the handheld computer into his mouth. He gripped the ladder and clambered down after Kay. The next level was much wider and brighter. Jake could hear music and voices coming from the surrounding walkways. Kay led him through a network of side passages and maintenance shafts.

'We're almost there,' she said. 'Not far now.'

The two of them spilled out on to a walkway full of people. Kay pointed to a low archway on the other side. Jake nodded and followed her through the crowd. A couple of traders waved fake crystals in his face. He pushed them aside and continued towards the opposite wall, where Kay was waiting. Jake could tell that something was wrong by her startled expression.

'Cutler,' snarled a savage voice.

Jake turned to find Scarabus Shark standing in the walkway. The oily-skinned pirate was holding his space helmet and a thick-bladed sword, which resembled a meat cleaver. His scarred face was a mixture of surprise and anger. The crowd scattered around them, not wishing to stand between Scarabus and his prey.

'I don't want to fight you,' said Jake, drawing the golden cutlass and backing towards the archway.

'I don't blame you,' laughed Scarabus, raising his weapon.

The space pirate captain attacked, swinging his sword like an axe. Jake dodged the thick blade and fought back with a thrust of his cutlass. Scarabus used his helmet to deflect the strike, before lashing out again with his sword. Jake blocked the blow, but the brute force of it knocked him off his feet.

'Is that all you've got?' Scarabus stood over Jake with the sword lifted above his head.

'Not so fast, fish face,' said Kay, whipping out a strange-looking pistol. 'Kid Cutler is with me.'

Scarabus bared his metal fangs. 'You dare to point that thing at me?'

'Aye,' she said, her finger stroking the trigger. 'Now drop your sword, before I blow your ugly head off.'

'You're messing with the wrong spacejacker.' Scarabus threw his weapon on to the metal grating and the walkway shook. 'I'll make you suffer for this, you little wretchards.'

'Kiss my cutlass,' said Kay, pulling the trigger.

'No,' shouted Jake, scrambling to his feet.

But instead of bullets, a cloud of bubbles squirted from the end of the barrel and popped on the pirate captain's face, leaving it covered in small wet circles. Scarabus looked furious at being tricked. He yelled with rage and lunged at them. Jake pulled Kay to the side and raised his cutlass.

'No you don't,' he said.

Scarabus glared at the blade pointed at his chest. Jake held it firm and kept his eyes on the pirate captain, as Kay tugged his arm.

'Come on,' she whispered. 'Let's go.'

The two of them darted through the archway and disappeared into the shadows before Scarabus could recover his sword. As they ran, Kay returned her pistol to its holster.

'Are you crazy?' exclaimed Jake. 'Who carries a toy gun in an illegal spaceport?'

'It's a semi-automatic bubble gun,' she corrected. 'And it was the first weapon that came to hand.'

Inside her jacket, Kay carried twin laser pistols with matching pearl handles, a cutlass, a stiletto dagger, throwing stars, a string of palm grenades and two feather dusters.

'Hey, this is where we left the ship,' said Jake, as they burst through an emergency exit in front of the docking bays.

Kay closed the door behind them and smashed the lock. 'We're not safe yet.'

Jake scanned the bays for the plump hull of the *Dark Horse*, but his eyes were drawn to a damaged space cutter, which had been recently patched up.

'That's the *Loose Cannon*,' he said, recognising Carla Gritt's ship.

'This way,' urged Kay, dragging him towards the bay where the *Dark Horse* was waiting.

The cargo hauler's loading ramp was down and two security guards lay sprawled at the bottom.

Jake spotted Nichelle on the bridge and knew that the crew were preparing to take off.

'Come with me,' he said. 'I'll give you a lift.'

'Thanks, but I've got my own ship.' Kay pointed to a neighbouring bay. 'Its hull is a little bashed, but it's still space-worthy.'

'The *Divine Wind*?'

'Yes, I'm its captain,' she said proudly. 'My crew call me Crazy Kay Jagger.'

'You're Wild Joe Jagger's daughter?'

Kay winked at him and Jake realised that the blood-red letter 'K' must stand for Kay. It had been her ship that had attacked the *ISS Magnificent*, allowing the *Dark Horse* to escape.

'I'll race you to the stars,' she said. 'The last one to leave the spaceport has scabby scurvy shorts.'

Before Jake could say another word, Kay ran off towards the *Divine Wind*. He shook his head in disbelief and headed for his own ship, but as he made his way to the old cargo hauler, a squad of security guards emerged from a different exit, led by Ormos.

'Get him,' roared the chief of security.

Jake sprinted towards the *Dark Horse* as a shower of bullets sparked off the bay floor around him. Amber lights flashed on the cargo hauler's hull and its engine rumbled. Kella and Nanoo were waiting on the loading ramp with Woorak, who provided cover fire with a machine gun.

'Hurry, Jake,' cried Kella.

'They coming fast,' warned Nanoo.

Jake could hear heavy bootsteps stomping closer. A bullet clipped his handheld computer, leaving a dent in its casing. He glanced across to the *Divine Wind* and was relieved to see Kay disappear inside the yellow star frigate. Woorak shouted something and pointed in the air. Jake looked up and saw that the robot parrot had escaped. It swooped down on him, its beak open wide.

Jake lashed out with the sword and clipped the bird, but it wasn't enough. The parrot sunk its razor-sharp talons into his chest. He cried out in pain and fell to the ground. The parrot sank its talons deeper and flapped its metal wings, scratching Jake's face with the serrated edges. In the background, the boot-steps drew nearer.

'Get off me,' shouted Jake, hitting the parrot with his handheld computer.

A shadow passed overhead and something collided with the robot, knocking it over. Jake swore out loud as the razor-sharp talons ripped from his flesh. He caught sight of two birds fighting behind him. Squawk the parrot had come to his rescue in a flurry of colourful feathers.

Ignoring the pain, Jake scurried across the floor with his head down. He reached the loading ramp and threw himself on to it. A second later, Squawk flew through the opening and landed on a container, cursing.

'It's t-t-time to go,' said Woorak, raising the ramp.

Kella and Nanoo helped Jake through the cargo hold and down the corridor to the guest quarters. As they leapt into their bunks and secured their straps, the *Dark Horse* pulled away from the docking bay. Jake heard bullets bouncing off the hull, like hailstones on a window.

'Is everyone OK?' asked Jake, the cuts on his chest making his eyes water.

'Yes,' said Kella. 'Kodan led us back through a series of secret security hatches.'

Jake quickly told them about his adventure with Kay and how she was the teenage captain of the *Divine Wind*.

'That's not all,' he said. 'I saw the *Loose Cannon*.'

'Are you sure?' asked Kella.

'Yes, I'm positive. I bet it was Carla Gritt who was watching Reus roulette with Captains Hawker and Shark.'

'How she survive?' asked Nanoo.

'I guess she was wearing a spacesuit inside her ship.'

Jake located his magnetic strips and re-attached them to the soles of his shoes. He then unfastened his straps and slid out of his bunk. His top was stained with blood and he struggled to walk as the cargo hauler powered towards the exit.

'Where are you going?' asked Kella.

'To the rear laser cannon,' he said. 'We still have Papa Don's fighter craft to get past and every laser bolt will count.'

Chapter 15

Gorks

Jake rushed to the captain's quarters and up the ladder to the rear turret. He entered the small compartment and straddled the laser cannon saddle. Nanoo had done a good job of rebuilding the damaged weapon, which looked the same as those on the gun deck. Jake powered it up and opened the gun port. A metal cover slid back and the cannon rolled forward. At the same moment, the *Dark Horse* burst free from the illegal spaceport, closely followed by the *Divine Wind*. Jake released the safety catch and scanned the stars for enemy craft.

'Where are you?' he muttered.

A torrent of laser bolts cut across the glass dome. Jake twisted on the saddle and spotted a wave of fighter craft. To his surprise, their hulls were not sleek and black but bulky and midnight blue, like chubby beetles with stubby wings.

'Gorks!' he cried, looking around for a way to contact the bridge, but there was no microphone in the turret, only a small speaker on the wall.

Jake had never met a Gork – or fin-head, as Woorak called them – but from what he knew, they would be shooting to kill. Their craft were larger than standard naval fighters and armed with twin laser cannon.

'Attention, crew,' said Farid over the intercom, which crackled with interference from the Tego Nebula. 'We've got incoming craft. I want everyone on battle stations. We'll have to fight our way out.'

Jake looked beyond the approaching Gork craft and spotted the *ISS Magnificent* in the distance. What was Admiral Vantard doing there?

'Let's do this,' he whispered to himself.

The laser cannon responded to his touch and rotated towards the cluster of fighter craft. Jake gripped the rubber handlebars and checked his display screen, which was also distorted by the nebula. He squinted his eyes, located the nearest Gork fighter and squeezed the trigger. If he thought asteroids were hard to hit, these craft were virtually impossible. His laser bolt curled out of the cannon as the *Dark Horse* changed direction, completely missing its intended target. He took aim at another fighter, but struggled to trap it in his sights.

'Keep still,' he shouted in frustration.

Maaka and Woorak seemed to be having more luck with the side cannon, picking off the nearest Gorks. The *Divine Wind* also managed to destroy two craft as it passed overhead. Jake gave up trying to aim his laser cannon and held down the trigger. He fired a series of laser bolts, in the hope that one of them would hit a passing fighter.

'Hold on, everyone,' shouted Nichelle over the intercom.

The *Dark Horse* dipped suddenly, before rising into a wide arc. Jake's laser bolts scattered behind the ship like a net over several of the fighters. He watched as one Gork swerved to avoid them and crashed into a neighbouring craft, while another tried to slip between the bolts, only to catch its wings and spin out of control.

'Magnifty,' he cheered, still squeezing the trigger.

'Jake, is that you back there?' said Granny Leatherhead through the small intercom speaker. 'There's a Gork gunship coming up fast behind us. I want you to take it out.'

Jake scanned the stars and located a vessel that looked like a giant cannon with wings. He swung his laser cannon around and took aim, but it refused to fire. A warning light flashed on the distorted display screen. His weapon had overheated.

'No,' he cried, thumping the hot metal.

The laser cannon hissed at him and powered down.

'What's going on, Jake?' asked Granny Leatherhead. 'That grotty gunship is gaining on us.'

Jake was unable to respond. He watched helplessly as the Gork vessel drew nearer. Why had he let his laser cannon overheat? Maaka had warned him that it might happen. He had been a fool to think that he was ready to be a gunner. The gunship fired a laser bolt the size of a cow, but Nichelle dodged it by pulling the *Dark Horse* into a steep climb before looping back behind their enemy. Kodan tore into its hull with Old Lizzy and the gunship exploded. The remaining Gork fighters retreated to a safe distance.

'That's enough fun for one day,' said Granny Leatherhead. 'Nichelle, set course for the sixth solar system and don't spare the boosters.'

'Aye, captain.'

'What about the *Divine Wind*?' asked Farid.

'Let them know where we're going,' said Granny Leatherhead. 'We need all the friends we can get right now, assuming they can keep up with us.'

'Aye, captain.'

Jake climbed down from the turret and headed to the bridge. His chest throbbed with pain as he entered the room.

'Well, well, if it isn't Kid Cutler,' mocked Granny Leatherhead. 'Did you forget how to shoot?'

'I'm sorry, captain,' he said. 'The Tego Nebula messed up my display and then my laser cannon overheated.'

'It's lucky for you that the rest of my crew know how to fight.' Granny Leatherhead glared at Papa Don's through the window. 'This is far from over. We're now on the run from the Interstellar Navy and the space mafia. I hope the sword is worth it.'

Jake glanced at the golden cutlass, which he had kept with him during the battle. If it helped him to convince the other leaders that he was the ruler of Altus, then it was worth it. But would the sword be enough to prevent a galactic war?

Jake sat in the dining area with Kella and Nanoo. It had been an hour since they had left the Tego Nebula and there was finally a decent stellar-net signal. He fiddled with his seat straps as the three of them watched the *Interstellar News*. The scrolling headline reported thirty-seven people dead in a clash between two ships: one from the United Worlds and the other from an independent colony.

'Is this linked to the stand-off over Vantos?' asked the newsreader.

'It's difficult to say,' said the reporter. 'No naval vessels were involved in the incident, but tensions continue to rise here in the seventh solar system. It's not clear why the two craft opened fire, except that crews are becoming increasingly suspicious of each other.'

'So we can expect to see further clashes of this nature?'

'Yes,' said the reporter. 'There's still no sign of the naval fleet leaving Vantos. A peaceful resolution seems less likely each day. We're also hearing reports of Gork ships terrorising independent cargo haulers and trading stations. It's as though the Interstellar Navy is intentionally trying to provoke a reaction.'

Kella reached up and turned down the volume. 'At least we're not at war yet.'

'I'll contact the mayor of Remota,' said Jake, activating his handheld computer. 'Hopefully he'll listen to me this time, now that I have the …'

'What up?' asked Nanoo.

Jake stared at the words on his screen.

'I've received an e-comm from Callidus.'

It was the first time that Jake had thought about Callidus and Capio since leaving Papa Don's. As he read the name, he realised how much he missed the fortune seeker. His finger tapped the screen and the e-comm opened.

'What's it say?' asked Kella.

'Callidus hopes that we're all safe and not too bored on Shan-Ti.' Jake followed the text with his finger. 'He says they have visited the canteen in the seventh solar system, where he was enlisted by the Interstellar Navy. According to the owner, Callidus was first dropped there over a decade ago by a crew of asteroid miners with no memories or belongings, nothing except his clothes and a few coins. Apparently, the owner let him work in the kitchen and sleep in the utility room, but Callidus was only there for three weeks before the Interstellar Navy signed him up for a six-year tour.'

Nanoo scrunched up his lilac face. 'Callidus was asteroid miner?'

'Yeah, it looks that way,' said Jake. 'He says that they have already tracked down the mining ship to the third solar system and they're on their way to find out more.'

Jake stopped reading. He had hoped that Callidus and Capio would be heading back to Shan-Ti by now, not going on another adventure without him. It would take them days to reach the third solar system, longer if they had to change ships, by which time the whole galaxy could be at war.

'Is that the end of the e-comm?' asked Kella.

Jake checked the screen. 'No, there's more. Callidus is worried about the incidents in the seventh solar system, which he says could escalate at any moment. He wants us to be careful and not take any risks.'

'Like visiting Papa Don's?' said Kella.

'Yeah, we had better not do that,' laughed Jake.

'Is there e-comm from cyber-monks?' asked Nanoo.

Jake checked the screen. 'No, nothing, why?'

'It OK,' said Nanoo. 'I wonder if they hear back from Taan-Centaur.'

Kella put her arm around Nanoo. 'Don't worry, I'm sure it won't be much longer before you can go home.'

'I hoping so, but first we stop war. Yes?'

Jake wrote a reply to Callidus, which covered everything that had happened since they had left Shan-Ti. This included visiting Baden Scott, stealing the sword of Altus from Papa Don, meeting Crazy Kay Jagger and their plan to prevent a galactic war. He hoped that Callidus and Capio would be able to meet them on Santanova for the gathering.

When Jake had finished, he located the contact details for the mayor of Remota and tapped the screen to connect.

'Here we go,' he said, as the device purred.

'Hello?' barked Hector Rumpole. 'This had better be important.'

Jake checked the clock and realised that it was still early on Remota.

'Good morning, mayor, I'm sorry to wake you,' he said. 'It's Jake Cutler; please don't hang up.'

Hector Rumpole seemed to consider this for a moment. 'What do you want, Jake?'

'I have the sword of Altus. It's a really old cutlass made of solid gold, which has been passed from ruler to ruler for centuries. The sword and the pendant both contain the symbol of Altus, proving that I'm not a liar. You must listen to me, mayor, the Interstellar Government is trying to start a galactic war and only we can stop it.'

There was another pause, followed by a deep sigh. 'I know.'

Jake, Kella and Nanoo looked at one another in surprise.

'You do?'

'Yes,' confessed the mayor. 'I'm sorry if I was a little harsh the last time we spoke. War is a grim business and not something that anyone wants to contemplate, but I've been watching the events unfold in the seventh solar system, and if there's an ounce of truth in what you're saying, the independent colonies are in grave danger.'

'Vantos is only the start,' said Jake. 'If we don't make a stand now, the Interstellar Government will take over the entire galaxy, one colony at a time.'

'Madness,' growled the mayor. 'Nobody turns Remota into a United Worlds planet.'

'That's exactly how I feel about Altus.'

'Altus,' echoed the mayor. 'So it does exist, then?'

'We found it a few months ago.'

'And it has a crystal moon?'

'Three of them,' said Jake.

The mayor whistled appreciatively. 'I used to dream about Altus as a boy. What's it like? Where did you find it?'

'It's the most beautiful planet in the seven solar systems,' boasted Jake. 'But I can't reveal its location until it's safe from the Interstellar Navy.'

'I understand,' said the mayor. 'If word got out, it would cause the biggest crystal rush in history. You keep your secret for now, while we find a way to stop this galactic war.'

'We have to warn the other leaders,' urged Jake. 'If we stand together, the Interstellar Navy will think twice before taking us all on.'

'OK, but it won't be easy,' said the mayor. 'I'll have to call a gathering of independent colony leaders. It will be the first one for decades, so it will attract a lot of attention. You'll need to convince them that you're the ruler of Altus and the threat is genuine, so you had better bring your crown and sword.'

'I don't have the crown.'

'It doesn't matter; wear any old crown. No one will know what it's supposed to look like anyway. At least your sword and pendant will look authentic.'

'Where will the gathering be held?' asked Jake.

'Keep watching the *Interstellar News*. They will want to report this historic event. The most central location is the fourth solar system. Therefore, I suggest planet Santanova, four days from now.'

'Thank you, mayor.'

'Yes, well, let's hope this does the trick.'

The call ended and Jake punched the air with excitement. It had worked: the mayor of Remota had taken him seriously. At last, they had found an ally who could help them to convince the other leaders. No one had ever managed to unite the independent colonies before, but surely the threat of galactic war would persuade them to join forces. Jake imagined himself appearing on the *Interstellar News* as the ruler of Altus.

Would his father be watching?

Chapter 16

The Supply Ship

'Let me get this straight,' said Kella. 'The entire Interstellar Navy is searching for the infamous Jake Cutler, but instead of hiding, you're going to speak at a major event watched by millions.'

Jake knew that he was taking a huge risk. If he failed to convince the other leaders that he was the ruler of Altus, he would end up in prison or handed over to Admiral Vantard.

'I have to do this,' he said. 'There's no other way. If the plan works, the other leaders will protect me and my planet from the Interstellar Navy. I reckon it's time that Altus stood by the rest of the independent colonies.'

'Is that your decision to make?' asked Kella. 'What about the Protectorate?'

Jake had met the Protectorate on Altus. It was a council of elders entrusted with keeping the planet a secret, by whatever means necessary. He had disobeyed them by helping the Space Dogs to escape.

'There's no way to contact them from outside the Tego Nebula and we can't risk returning there,' said Jake. 'Besides, if we unite the independent colonies, there will be no need to keep Altus a secret. We can sign a treaty to keep its crystal moons safe from the Galactic Trade Corporation. I don't have to tell anyone its location. At least, not at first.'

Nanoo stood up. 'Let us go tell the captain.'

'I'm sure she'll be thrilled to return to the fourth solar system,' said Kella. 'You know how much she likes that big red sun.'

Jake, Kella and Nanoo scurried up to the bridge to tell the captain about the call with Hector Rumpole.

'The fourth solar system, eh?' mused Granny Leatherhead. 'We had better take the scenic route if we want to avoid the Interstellar Navy and the space mafia. Papa Don will be looking for his family sword.'

Jake was pleased to see the captain back in command of the *Dark Horse*. In a strange way, the time away from the ship had done her good. Her skin looked healthier and her single grey eye sparkled. If it hadn't been for Kella, the captain would still be sick, or perhaps even dead.

'I know a few routes we can take,' said Nichelle.

'Good, I hoped you might.' Granny Leatherhead hoisted her thumb at the side window, where the *Divine Wind* still flanked them. 'Farid, you had better see if the barmy bunch want to join us.'

'I don't think we could shake them if we wanted to,' said the first mate. 'Their captain has taken a shine to Jake.'

'Miss Jagger?' Granny Leatherhead humphed. 'Who could blame her when Jake, sorry, Captain Cutler, single-handedly destroyed the *ISS Colossus* and evaded the entire Interstellar Navy. I expect that she'll explode when he saves the whole galaxy.'

Jake ignored her. He couldn't help it if people assumed that he was in charge of the *Dark Horse*.

'Captain,' said Farid. 'I'm picking up something on the scanners.'

'That's the *Divine Wind*,' she grumped.

'No, there's another vessel. It's a Galactic Trade Corporation supply ship.'

'What's that doing out here?' wondered the captain. 'Is it guarded?'

Farid checked the long-range scanner. 'No, it's travelling alone.'

'Then what are we waiting for?' asked Granny Leatherhead. 'Battle stations, everyone, we've got work to do.'

Jake glanced at the display screen and caught sight of a small midnight blue craft. It was long and thin like a bullet, with no side windows or gun ports, only a single laser cannon turret.

'We don't have time to do any spacejacking,' he protested. 'Not when we have a galactic war to stop.'

'Your gathering will have to wait,' said Granny Leatherhead. 'We're almost out of food and we need more fuel cells. If we're lucky, they might be carrying a crate of crystals. I reckon it would do you space pups good to join the boarding party.'

'But –'

Who's in charge here?' thundered Granny Leatherhead. 'I said battle stations!'

'Aye, captain.'

Jake, Kella and Nanoo stood in the airlock behind Farid, Maaka and Woorak. The three teenagers wore oversized combat suits and kit belts, which Manik had adjusted for them, as well as silver skull-shaped space helmets stuffed with extra padding. Jake knew how odd they looked in the loose-fitting outfits, but that was the least of their worries.

'Hey, Farid,' said Jake. 'I've been meaning to ask you about something.'

'What is it?'

'Why doesn't James Hawker like you?'

'What makes you think that?' asked the first mate.

'He suggested that you play Reus roulette.'

'Oh,' said Farid. 'I used to serve under him on the *Lost Soul*, before I joined the Space Dogs. Captain Hawker never forgave me for switching crews. He expects the Starbucklers to remain loyal, which makes me a traitor in his eyes.'

'Why did you leave?' asked Jake.

'Granny Leatherhead offered me a promotion. I think she only did it to make him angry.'

'Why would anyone want to upset James Hawker?'

The intercom crackled.

'Brace yourselves, boarding party,' said Granny Leatherhead. 'We're coming into firing range.'

Jake heard the unmistakable sound of Old Lizzy spewing out laser bolts as the *Dark Horse* swooped down on the supply ship. He peered through the airlock window and caught sight of the *Divine Wind* flying alongside them with its pink cannon blasting. The aim was not to hit the supply ship, only to scare its crew. But then something bright flashed past the airlock window.

'Those corporate creeps are firing back,' screeched Granny Leatherhead. 'Kodan, wipe out that laser cannon. Nichelle, take evasive action.'

'Aye, captain.'

The cargo hauler lurched to the side, causing Jake to bump into Nanoo. There were several more bursts from Old Lizzy before the multi-barrelled laser cannon fell silent.

'Good work, Kodan,' said Granny Leatherhead. 'They've cut their engine. Nichelle, move us closer.'

'Aye, captain.'

Amber lights flashed on the ceiling of the airlock.

'Warning, airlock door opening,' announced the speaker on the wall.

Jake stowed his weapons and checked his lifeline. His heart raced as he thought about leaping into space. Who knew what was waiting for them inside the supply ship. Scargus had told him that no job was without risk – there was always a chance that someone would get hurt. His space dock fantasies of being a swashbuckling space pirate seemed so naive now.

The huge airlock door cracked open and the oxygen escaped through the gap. Jake held on to a wall strap to steady himself. He could tell that the *Dark Horse* was still moving by the stars flying past the opening. The *Divine Wind* drew level and Jake caught sight of Kay standing in her airlock with her boarding party. He smiled at her pink skull-shaped space helmet, yellow combat suit and knee-length space boots. Around her waist she wore a lace tutu and in her hand she waved a feather duster.

'That g-g-girl really is crazy,' stuttered Woorak.

The *Dark Horse* slowed and the supply ship appeared below them. Jake spotted a gnarled black stump where the laser cannon had been positioned. Farid attached his lifeline to the spare tow cable and jumped into space feet first. Maaka and Woorak followed, brandishing their swords as they slid through the stars.

Jake was next to attach his lifeline to the tow cable. He kicked off the edge of the airlock and hurled himself into space, spiralling towards the supply ship below. Through the protective mesh that covered his eyes, Jake spotted a second tow cable. Kay slid confidently into view ahead of her shipmates.

Farid, Maaka and Woorak were the first to reach the metal surface. Jake squeezed the tow cable with his padded gloves to reduce his speed. He landed heavily with a magnetic thud and unclipped his lifeline. Kella and Nanoo touched down moments later, followed by Kay and the Luna Ticks. Woorak had already started work on the airlock with his laser cutter.

'Ahoy-hoy,' said Kay, skipping across the hull with a string of palm grenades in her hand. 'A laser cutter will take too long, let's blast it open.'

Farid held up his hands. 'No way, those things are too unpredictable. If we damage the airlock door, we won't be able to enter the ship. It's safer to remove the control panel.'

'Spoilsport,' said Kay, wrapping the string of palm grenades around her waist.

Jake watched the laser cutter eat into the thick metal surface. After a few minutes, a small panel toppled into space and Woorak opened the airlock door. Maaka drew his laser pistol and entered, followed by Farid and Woorak. Jake, Kella and Nanoo joined them in the narrow airlock. Kay was the last to squeeze inside, before the outer door closed and the compartment filled with oxygen.

'Is everyone ready?' asked Farid.

Jake, Kella and Nanoo drew their weapons.

Farid opened the inner airlock door and tossed out a smoke grenade. He waited for a few seconds and then charged after it with Maaka and Woorak. A medley of shouts and laser fire broke out. Jake,

Kella, Nanoo and Kay stepped cautiously into the smoke-filled corridor, where visibility was limited.

'This way,' said Jake, heading towards the shouting.

A stray laser bolt tore through the smoke and glanced off his helmet, knocking him backwards. He dropped to the floor and came face to face with a damaged robot, which lay twitching on its side with several holes in its chest plate. The smoke cleared and Farid came charging up the corridor.

'We've taken the ship,' he said.

Jake looked past him and saw more robots strewn along the corridor. 'Where are all the people?'

Maaka laughed. 'Do you really think that the Galactic Trade Corporation would pay people when they can use cheap robots to deliver their supplies?'

Jake stood up and regarded the damaged robot with a mixture of fear and pity. He knew it was just a machine, but it reminded him of the battle droid Vigor-8. Sparks sputtered from its broken body and the robot stopped moving. Jake watched its lights fade and he knew that it had ceased operating.

With no time to waste, the boarding party entered the capacious cargo hold, but there wasn't much left to steal.

Kay glanced around the sparse walls. 'What, no crystals?'

'It doesn't look like it,' said Farid. 'If this ship was carrying any treasure, it has already been dropped off.'

'Let's just t-t-take what's left,' stuttered Woorak.

'I'll carry some food,' said Kella.

'And I get fuel cells,' volunteered Nanoo.

Jake picked up a crate of drinks and turned to the door, but as he did so, a robot guard limped into the cargo hold, clutching a laser pistol. Its leg was damaged and one of its arms was missing, but it was still functioning and programmed to kill.

'Look out,' cried Jake, dropping the crate and reaching for his gun.

The robot fired first, narrowly missing Kay. Jake took aim and blasted the robot with three laser bolts to the head. It collapsed in a smoking heap of metal and wires. The shots echoed and faded, leaving an eerie silence.

'That was close,' said Farid. 'Nice shooting, Jake.'

Before he could reply, the captain's voice flooded their helmets.

'Attention, boarding party,' she croaked. 'We've got incoming craft on the long-range scanner. Leave the supply ship and get your butts back here on the double.'

Jake could tell by her tone that she was worried.

'Aye, captain,' said Farid.

'What about supplies?' asked Nanoo.

'Grab food, drink and fuel, but leave the rest.'

The seven of them quickly attached a variety of bags, bottles and boxes to their combat suits and headed to the airlock.

'What are you lot waiting for?' screeched Granny Leatherhead. 'There's a squadron of Gork fighters heading this way. If you're not back inside this cargo hauler within five minutes, I'm leaving without you.'

Chapter 17

Space Battle

Farid, Maaka, Woorak and Kay entered the narrow airlock.

'There's no more room,' complained Kella. 'It's not big enough for all of us and the supplies.'

'It's OK,' said Jake. 'Let them go first.'

Farid nodded and closed the inner door.

As it slid shut, Kay threw her feather duster to Jake and shouted, 'It's for luck.'

Jake caught the duster and the door sealed. He heard the outer hatch open and then close again a moment later. It took another minute for the oxygen levels to restore before they could finally open the inner door.

'This is taking too long,' said Kella anxiously.

Nanoo checked his wrist computer. 'We have only three minutes to get back to the *Dark Horse*.'

Jake, Kella and Nanoo entered the airlock and closed the inner door. A few seconds later, the outer door opened and they were scrambling back across the hull to the tow cable.

'Look,' said Nanoo, pointing into space. 'Gork fighter craft.'

Jake peered through the protective mesh and spotted at least twenty shapes speeding towards them. He checked the tow cable and saw that the others had almost reached the ship.

'How long do we have left?' he asked, connecting his lifeline to the thick wire.

'Just over a minute,' said Nanoo. 'It not enough time to climb tow cable.'

Jake refused to give up. 'There has to be a way.'

'We'll never make it,' said Kella. 'The *Dark Horse* is too far away.'

Jake glanced at the approaching Gork fighters and then at the feather duster in his hand. Why was he still holding the wretched thing? What was he supposed to do with it, tickle the enemy? It looked ridiculous, like a little nebula cloud on a stick.

'That's it,' he said. 'Do you remember how Callidus and Capio used compressed air to propel themselves through the Tego Nebula? We can use our oxygen tanks in the same way.'

'Don't we need them to breathe?' asked Kella.

'We'll still have a bit left in our combat suits once we disconnect the tanks.' Jake tucked the feather duster into his belt. 'It should be enough for two or three breaths.'

'If we link suits, we need only one oxygen tank,' suggested Nanoo.

'Good idea,' said Jake.

Kella and Nanoo attached their lifelines to his belt.

'Whose tank are we going to use?' asked Kella.

'It was my idea, so we'll use mine,' said Jake. 'And there's no time to argue.'

Ignoring their objections, Jake took a deep breath and disconnected the metal canister. He flipped it over and pointed the nozzle at the hull of the supply ship. It took him three attempts to open the valve before a jet of compressed air exploded from the end. He locked his fingers around the tank as it blasted into space, dragging the three of them behind it.

'Hold on,' he said, using up his first breath.

Jake's lifeline scraped along the tow cable in a shower of sparks as they rocketed towards the *Dark Horse*. Farid, Maaka and Woorak were watching them from the edge of the airlock.

'It working,' cried Nanoo.

The Gork fighters were closer now and Jake could make out their chubby midnight blue hulls. He took his second breath when they reached the half-way point and was surprised to find that the oxygen had already thinned inside his combat suit. It made him feel light-headed and his fingers loosened around the metal canister.

'We're almost there,' encouraged Kella.

Jake's head was spinning and his vision started to blur. He could make out amber lights flashing above the open airlock door.

'It's going to shut,' he wheezed. 'It's going to …'

'We can make it,' said Kella.

'I …'

The universe became distorted and shrouded in a thick fog. Jake felt the oxygen tank wriggle free and slip through his fingers, but he was too weak to catch it. His whole body numbed and before he could stop himself, he lost consciousness.

When Jake stirred, he was strapped into a bed in the medical bay. At first, he thought there was something wrong with his eye implants, but then he realised the lights were red. His lungs expanded with stale oxygen and something rumbled in the distance. It took him a moment to remember what had happened. How did they get back aboard? A sharp headache swirled around his skull as the *Dark Horse* rocked from side to side. What was that rumbling noise? It sounded like explosions and laser cannon fire ... the space battle had started.

Jake unclipped his straps and tumbled into the air.

'Where are you going?' asked Kella, entering the room with an armful of blankets.

'I need to get to the rear cannon,' he said. 'What happened outside the ship? How did we get back inside?'

'You passed out and let go of the oxygen tank, but Nanoo caught the nozzle and steered us into the airlock.'

'Nanoo? Magnifty.' Jake scanned the floor. 'Where are my gravity shoes?'

'Jake, you've had a nasty –'

'I'm fine,' he lied. 'I've got to help defend the ship. Where are my ... oh, forget it.'

Jake pushed himself off a cabinet and floated through the open door. It had been a while since he had negotiated his way through the ship without gravity shoes and his arms ached by the time he reached the top deck. Without knocking, he entered the captain's quarters, flew across her bed and climbed into the rear turret.

Jake gripped the laser cannon saddle with his knees and powered up the weapon. The gun port slid back and the cannon rolled forward. Jake was greeted by splashes of bright light, like a deadly firework display. Gork fighters weaved around fragments of wreckage, firing their twin laser cannon, while Nichelle plunged the *Dark Horse* into deep rolls.

'No more mistakes, Kid Cutler,' he said to himself.

His body tensed as he released the safety catch and gripped the rubber handlebars. The Gork fighters were as fast as ever, but at least this time his display screen worked. Jake picked his first target and squeezed the trigger. The laser cannon fired and the Gork craft exploded.

'One down,' he muttered.

A pair of Gork fighters tore past the turret, blasting the cargo hauler's shields on either side of him. Jake spun his laser cannon around and fired a series of short bursts, catching one of the crafts and knocking out its engine. In the distance, the *Divine Wind* lost one of its gun ports as it collided with a damaged fighter.

Two more Gorks swooped down on the *Dark Horse*, their weapons blazing. Jake returned fire, but he was careful not to overheat his laser cannon.

His shots took out one of the fighters and damaged the other. The cargo hauler's shields had weakened and its hull had gained several new scars.

'Right, that's it, we're leaving,' said Granny Leatherhead. 'Kodan, clear a path for us. Nichelle, set course for the fourth solar system as planned.'

'Aye, captain.'

Kodan finished off a damaged fighter and Nichelle resumed course to the fourth solar system, closely followed by the *Divine Wind*. Jake scanned the stars for more targets. It was up to him to cover their rear and he was not going to let down the crew. He picked off the pursuing craft one at a time, as though he were playing a stellar-net game. His confidence grew with each shot and it wasn't long before the last of the Gork fighters fell back.

'That's it,' cheered Farid. 'We're in the clear.'

'Nice shooting, Kid Cutler,' said Granny Leatherhead over the intercom. 'We'll make a gunner out of you yet.'

Jake paced the guest quarters while Kella and Nanoo rested on their beds. It was nearly three days until the gathering and there was a lot to think about.

'I'm going to wear my Altian uniform,' he said. 'It will go well with the seal and sword of Altus.'

'What about the missing crown?' asked Kella.

'I'll ask Scargus to make me one out of scrap metal and spray it with gold paint. It won't be perfect, but it will be better than nothing.'

'What you say to other leaders?' asked Nanoo.

'That's a good question.' Jake remembered how Hector Rumpole had reacted at the mention of a galactic war. 'I need to write a speech.'

Jake had tried public speaking on Altus. He had stood in front of huge crowds, reading out messages written for him by professional speech-writers. Most of these had gone OK, but none of them were as important as the speech he had to deliver at the gathering.

Jake rummaged in his bag for some pens and paper, which the cyber-monks on Shan-Ti had given him. He got to work on the opening line of his speech over the next hour, but the words did not come easily.

'You need more about Altus,' said Nanoo, looking over his shoulder. 'You not explained it real.'

'My head hurts.' Jake scooped up the paper. 'Let's take a break and go to the engine room.'

The three of them made their way up the corridor to visit Scargus and Manik.

'Hello, Space Pups,' said Scargus, his hands wrapped around a flask of pirate tea. 'How's it going?'

Jake held out a piece of paper with a drawing on it. 'Can you make me this?'

Scargus took the sketch. 'A crown?'

'Yes, I need one for the gathering.'

'I could probably knock up something out of spare parts,' said the engineer, squinting at the design. 'But it won't be anything fancy, no jewels or engravings, like in your picture.'

'Thanks, I knew that I could count on you.' Jake held up another piece of paper. 'Now all I need is a speech. Any ideas?'

'Sorry, Jakey-boy, I can't help you there,' said Scargus. 'I never was any good with words.'

Jake turned to Manik.

'Don't look at me,' she said. 'I'm rubbish at public speaking. I tried to make a speech once, when I was training to be a mechanic. It was for the graduation ceremony and I had to stand up in front of all the other students and their families. I spent weeks preparing for it, but instead of sticking to my notes, I panicked and ended up rambling on and on and … Oh, there I go again, talking too much.'

Jake wished that Callidus was there, because he would know what to say. It wasn't about using fancy language or sounding good on the *Interstellar News*. The speech had to be right, otherwise no one would take him seriously. If he failed to convince the independent colonies to unite, they would be picked off one at a time by the Interstellar Navy, until there were none left. The fate of the galaxy now rested on his words.

Chapter 18

The Truth about Kid Cutler

'Jake, wake up,' shouted Nanoo.

'What's going on?'

Jake had fallen asleep working on his speech. He woke up in his room, floating inches from the ceiling, immersed in a cloud of pens and paper.

'*Interstellar News*,' said Nanoo, standing in the doorway. 'It talk about gathering.'

Jake rubbed his tired eyes and located his gravity shoes. His breath smelt of stale biscuits and he needed a wash, but there was no time to freshen up. He scrambled out of his room and up to the dining area on the first deck, where several of the crew were gathered in front of a display screen. They were watching a reporter standing outside a large, ornate building under a smoky red sky.

'... but the mayor of Remota is still refusing to say why he has called this historic event. As we heard earlier, it's the first gathering of independent colony leaders in over twenty years. The last time they met was to agree the price of crystals, which helped to avoid another mega-depression.'

'The timing of this gathering would suggest it's related to the Vantos situation,' speculated the newsreader. 'Are the United Worlds concerned?'

'No one from the Interstellar Government has been available for comment,' said the reporter. 'But if this is related to the increasing tensions in the seventh solar system, it's difficult to determine what the mayor of Remota is hoping to achieve. As we heard earlier, the Interstellar Navy has now given Vantos, Abbere and Torbana three days to apologise, or face the consequences. That's three days, which is how long we have until the gathering. A few of the independent colony leaders have played down the meeting, claiming that Hector Rumpole only wants to discuss crystal tax or trade route security. It's even been suggested that the gathering is nothing more than a media stunt to boost tourism on Remota.'

'Well, it has certainly captured our interest, thanks, Tom.' The newsreader turned to face the camera. 'In other news, a Galactic Trade Corporation ship was attacked today by space pirates –'

'Is that it?' said Jake. 'Did they say where on Santanova the gathering would be held?'

Maaka nodded. 'It's going to be in the capital city of Lugar.'

'It will take us almost three d-d-days to get to the f-f-fourth solar system,' stuttered Woorak. 'Nichelle had b-b-better hurry.'

'We need to let the captain know,' said Jake, heading for the door with Kella and Nanoo.

Scargus called after them. 'Tell her that there will be news crews and enhanced security.'

The three of them reached the top deck before they realised that something was wrong.

'Hey,' said Nanoo. 'Why ship slow down?'

The noise of the engine had reduced to a mechanical murmur. Jake wondered if they had run into more Gork fighters or perhaps a fortune seeker, but there were no explosions or laser cannon fire.

'What's going on?' he asked, as they entered the bridge.

'We're stopping for repairs,' said Granny Leatherhead.

'But there's no time. We have to get to Santanova.'

'Santanova?' laughed Granny Leatherhead. 'If we don't patch up these old ships, we won't make it to the next service port.'

Jake glanced out of the side window at the *Divine Wind*. The yellow star frigate was in a bad way.

Apart from extensive damage to its hull, the ship had only one working engine and a couple of gun ports left. It seemed to limp towards them, barely able to hold a straight course.

'We're going to connect our airlocks,' explained Farid. 'Kay contacted us a few minutes ago. Apparently, they have a medical emergency and their medic only knows basic first aid.'

'I'll go and fetch my medical kit,' said Kella.

Jake and Nanoo told the captain about the gathering and the Interstellar Navy's deadline, before heading back downstairs. As they reached the bottom deck, Jake heard the *Divine Wind* connect with the *Dark Horse*. Kella was already waiting by the inner airlock door.

'Do you know who's hurt?' he asked.

'No,' she said.

The door opened and standing in the airlock was Crazy Kay Jagger, supported by one of her shipmates. Her skin was porcelain white and her sweaty pink hair clung to her bruised face. A thick bloodstained bandage was wrapped tightly around her thigh. As she caught sight of Jake, a smile trembled on her scarlet lips.

'Kay!' he exclaimed. 'What happened?'

The teenage pirate captain limped into the corridor.

'Ahoy-hoy, mates,' she said, weakly. 'We were repairing a damaged laser cannon when it exploded. I was hit by some shrapnel and was lucky not to lose my leg. Can you help me? My medic has fainted.'

Jake sat with Kay in the dining area of the *Dark Horse*. Kella had used the pendant to stop the bleeding and she was now cleaning up the medical bay while Scargus, Manik and Nanoo helped to patch up the *Divine Wind*. Kay had a fresh bandage and she was recovering with a flask of sweet pirate tea.

'Why do you do it?' asked Jake. 'Why do you put yourself in danger to help us?'

Kay smiled. 'It's the sort of thing my dad would have done.'

Jake glanced at the cuts and bruises on her face. 'But you could get killed.'

'I nearly did,' she said and her smile faltered. 'A few of the shipmates were killed in the explosion and the rest are not happy about it. My first mate reckons that the crew will mutiny if we don't start making some money soon. He says they won't keep risking their lives for free, not even for the Space Dogs.'

'Well, I think it's great that you want to help other pirate crews.'

'Thanks, matey.' Kay hid behind her flask. 'I just wish that I was half as good a spacejacker as you.'

'Me?'

'Yes, you,' she said and her eyes flashed with excitement. 'Kid Cutler, the teenage space pirate who defeated a super-destroyer using only his courage and a rusty old cargo hauler. I know all about you, Jake. How the Interstellar Navy burned down your monastery on Remota, but you escaped and hunted down Admiral Nex to make him pay.'

Now it was Jake's turn to hide behind his flask. 'You make me sound like a hero.'

'There's no need to be modest. I've read all of the Kid Cutler stories on the stellar-net. How many other pirate captains have blown up a kalmar or escaped from a black hole? Your adventures inspired me to repair my father's ship and seek out a new crew.'

Jake mumbled something into his drink.

'What did you say?'

'I'm not a pirate captain,' he said, looking up. 'I never was and I didn't do those half of the things you've mentioned. At least, not on my own.'

'I don't understand?'

'Granny Leatherhead is the captain of the *Dark Horse*,' he said. 'I'm only a trainee gunner.'

'A trainee gunner?' Kay looked confused. 'I don't understand. Is that meant to be a joke?'

'I'm afraid not.'

'You mean it's all lies?' Her hand moved dangerously close to her laser pistols. 'Is none of it true? Not even the *ISS Colossus*?'

'No – I mean, yes – well, sort of.' Jake put down his flask. 'Let me tell you what really happened, my story, the truth about Kid Cutler.'

It took Jake the best part of an hour to tell Kay his story. He described growing up on Remota, the monastery attack, his escape aboard the *Dark Horse*, the crystal hunters in Papa Don's, saving Kella from slavery, rescuing Nanoo from a shipwreck, being arrested by the Interstellar Navy, the kalmar attack, the battle of the black hole and finding his home planet. By the time he reached the part about leaving Altus, Kay was hanging on his every word.

'Hah,' she laughed. 'Just a trainee gunner, eh? You had me going there for a minute.'

'But that part is true,' he said.

'Yeah, I know, but you're not any old gunner, are you? How many spacejackers are also the ruler of a planet?'

Jake grinned. 'You know what, I actually miss Altus. It may have been colonised by pirates, but most of the people there are now farmers and fishermen. The capital city, Karmadon, looks beautiful in the ruby moonset. It even has a Great Hall made out of solid gold.'

Kay's sapphire blue eyes sparkled. 'That sounds amazing.'

'Yeah, it's pretty magnifty. I'd like to return there when I find my dad.'

Kella entered the dining area and strapped herself into a seat. 'Is there any tea?'

Jake fetched her a fresh flask. 'You look exhausted.'

'I feel it,' she moaned, taking the drink. 'You try cleaning the medical bay in zero gravity. Blood gets everywhere.'

'Sorry about the mess,' said Kay. 'But thanks for sorting out my leg.'

'Hey, no problem.' Kella smiled. 'We spacejackers have got to stick together, right?'

Kay laughed. 'You? A spacejacker? With an accent like that? Jake told me you were from a United Worlds planet.'

Kella's face crumbled. 'I don't know *who* I am any more.'

Kay looked startled. 'What did I say?'

'Kella was born a United Worlds citizen,' said Jake. 'But now she's a spacejacker and a ship's medic.'

'Am I?' Kella's tired eyes filled with angry tears. 'It doesn't sound as though I belong anywhere. I always wanted to be a doctor and help people, but crystal healing is banned on the United Worlds. Now I'm too posh to be a pirate.'

Jake reached for her hand. 'A friend once told me that it doesn't matter who you were or where you came from, but who you are now and where you want to be. And she was right.'

Kella rubbed her eyes with shaking palms. 'Your friend sounds like a smart girl.'

Jake laughed. 'The smartest. Not to mention a first-class spacejacker.'

'It's funny,' she sniffed. 'I've lived in my sister's shadow my whole life. My parents were so pleased when she took over the family crystal mine. But all this time, Jeyne has been plotting to take down the Interstellar Government. Now I'm helping to unite the independent colonies. My parents will never forgive either of us for betraying the United Worlds.'

'At least you have parents,' said Kay bluntly.

Jake decided to change the subject, before the pink-haired pirate could upset Kella further. 'How are the repairs going?'

Kay shrugged, but she took the hint. 'I suppose I'd better go and check on my crew. Thanks again for healing my leg, Kella. I'll catch you later, boy ruler.'

Kella frowned at Jake as Kay limped out of the door. 'You told her about Altus?'

'I didn't tell her the location,' he said. 'What's it matter anyway? In a few days' time, I'm going to tell the entire galaxy that Altus exists.'

'Does that mean you've finished your speech?'

'Nearly,' he said, but this wasn't strictly true. 'In fact, I have a couple more ideas that I need to write down, so I'll see you later.'

Jake wandered back to his room, where his half-written speech was scattered in the air. He fetched down the scribbled notes and sorted them into the right order. As he read the words, he hoped they were good enough to convince the other leaders of the danger.

'You can do this,' he told himself. 'You have to do this. There's no one else coming to the rescue.'

Jake opened his cabinet and pulled out his belongings. If he looked like a leader, he might feel like one. His Altian uniform was rolled up inside an old blanket, along with the sword of Altus. He carefully unpacked it and started to change. It had been a few months since he had last worn the maroon jacket and the collar felt strange around his neck.

He slid the sword into its sheath and checked his reflection in the porthole window. The face that looked back seemed older and more serious than he remembered.

'My name is Jake Cutler,' he said confidently. 'And I am the ruler of Altus.'

Chapter 19

Dog Fight

Jake was relieved when the crew had finished patching up the *Divine Wind* and the two ships were on their way to the fourth solar system. Vantos remained surrounded by naval warships, refusing to apologise as the deadline approached. It was a stand-off while the galaxy waited for the gathering.

Jake had spent the day in his quarters, working on the remainder of his speech and checking his handheld computer for messages. Nanoo was building a new gadget in the engine room while Kella pottered about the medical bay. It seemed that all three of them needed some time alone.

As for the rest of the crew, Granny Leatherhead seemed stronger and claimed that she had never felt better. Nichelle, Farid and Kodan were taking it in turns to sleep, so there was always someone to pilot the ship and watch the scanners. Maaka and Woorak stayed close to the laser cannon on the gun deck while Manik looked after the engine.

Scargus was busy creating a crown for the gathering, which he had fashioned by bolting shards of rusted metal on to a section of old pipe. The last time Jake had checked, it had looked more like a torture device than a crown.

'It's not finished yet,' the chief engineer had told him. 'It still needs a bit of tidying up and a splat of paint.'

Jake had tried to appear pleased, but he secretly dreaded the thought of wearing such a crude-looking crown in front of the other leaders. No one would take him seriously with that pile of junk on his head.

It was now only two days until the gathering and Jake had nearly finished his speech. He was happy with everything except the ending, which needed to be perfect. His eyes were tired and his brain ached, so he decided to take a break. He snatched the handheld computer out of the air and saw that there was an e-comm from Callidus. With a flick of his finger, he opened the message and quickly read the words, as though worried they might disappear without warning:

Ahoy, Jake. Capio and I caught a fast ship to the third solar system and we're on our way to meet the captain of the mining crew. I was surprised to hear about Papa

Don's and the gathering of leaders. Don't get me wrong, I'm proud of you for taking action and it sounds as though you're doing the right thing, but I'm worried about your safety. Capio and I will join you on Santanova as soon as we can. In the meantime, keep an eye on the stars and stay out of trouble. Callidus.

Why was that last line so familiar? Callidus often said it, but where else had Jake read those words recently? He repeated them out loud.

'Keep an eye on the stars and stay out of trouble.'

Jake had seen the exact same phrase in Papa Don's illegal spaceport. He remembered reading it on a plaque outside Papa Don's quarters. Was it something to do with the space mafia? Had Callidus worked for them in the past?

The intercom crackled.

'Attention, crew,' said Granny Leatherhead. 'We've got incoming ships on the long-range scanner. Farid reckons they're not naval vessels, but I'm not taking any chances. I want everyone on battle stations.'

Jake rushed up to the top deck, but instead of heading to the rear turret, he made his way to the front of the ship. He had a bad feeling about the approaching craft and he wanted to see them for himself. As he entered the bridge, he caught sight of the three ships on the main display screen.

'What is it, Kid Cutler?' asked Granny Leatherhead.

'I've seen those ships before,' he said.

'Where?'

'I don't know, but there's something familiar about their shapes.'

'Stop wasting my time,' she snapped. 'I want you up in that turret, covering our rear.'

'Captain,' interrupted Farid. 'I've identified the ships.'

'Well?' she said. 'Who are they?'

'It's the *Lost Soul*, the *Black Death* and the *Loose Cannon*.'

'Grubber me,' she exclaimed. 'You had better warn the Luna Ticks.'

'Why is Carla Gritt hanging out with Captains Hawker and Shark?' asked Jake.

'That's what I would like to know,' said Granny Leatherhead. 'I don't trust any of those wretchards.'

'Can we outrun them?'

'If we use the new boosters,' said Farid. 'But I doubt the *Divine Wind* could keep up.'

Jake shook his head. 'We should stick together.'

'What's more important?' asked Granny Leatherhead. 'Getting you to the gathering, or helping that potty-mouthed pirate girl and her crackpot crew?'

'We're not leaving Kay behind,' he insisted. 'How many times has she risked her life to save us?'

Granny Leatherhead scowled at the approaching vessels on the display screen.

'OK, fine,' she said. 'We'll find out what they want, but this ship had better be ready to scarper the moment there's any trouble. Now get your butt into that turret, Kid Cutler, that's an order.'

'Aye, captain.'

Jake hurried to the rear laser cannon and quickly activated it. The *Dark Horse* was being pursued by two of the most feared pirate crews to ever roam the seven solar systems, as well as a devious fortune seeker. What chance did the Space Dogs have against the Starbucklers and the Crimson Hulls? The only pirate more notorious than James Hawker and Scarabus Shark was Jake.

'Ahoy, space slackers,' hailed Scarabus, his voice grating through the intercom speakers.

'Ahoy, tin teeth,' said Granny Leatherhead. 'You're a long way from Papa Don's. What do you want?'

'The golden cutlass, the pendant and that slippery little thief, Jake Cutler. Hand him over and we'll let you live, but resist and we'll scuttle your worthless hulls. I've already alerted the Interstellar Navy. Admiral Vantard is on his way to pick up the boy.'

'How dare you threaten my crew,' snarled Granny Leatherhead. 'You always were too big for your gravity boots, Scarabus Shark.'

'It's not personal, Lizzy,' said James Hawker. 'We've been after Jake for a while now. He's drawing too much attention and he needs to be stopped. We tried to trap him in the fifth solar system, but he got away, thanks to Kay Jagger.'

'Was that why Admiral Vantard was at Papa Don's?' asked Granny Leatherhead. 'I bet you invited him the moment we blundered through your door.'

'None of that matters now,' said Scarabus. 'This is your last chance. Hand over Jake Cutler or we'll blow you to stardust.'

'No deal,' shouted Crazy Kay, on behalf of both crews. 'We're not going anywhere, you snivelling sons of snitches. If you lay a finger on either of our ships, I'll rip off your arms and slap you with them.'

'Ahoy there, little miss crazy,' said Scarabus. 'I was hoping you would stick around, because I still owe you for that bubble gun stunt you pulled in Papa Don's.'

'What are you going to do?' sneered Kay. 'Teach me a lesson? What makes you think that you could beat the *Divine Wind*?'

'It wouldn't be the first time,' said Scarabus.

The communicator fell silent.

'So, it was you who killed Wild Joe Jagger,' croaked Granny Leatherhead. 'I've always had my suspicions, but there was never any proof. What did he ever do to you?'

'Joe was out of control,' said Scarabus. 'He was bad for business and I didn't want to see his treasure wasted.'

There was a long silence. Jake waited for Kay to scream or shout, but instead she spoke slowly and deliberately into her communicator.

'Kiss. My. Cutlass.'

And with that, the *Divine Wind* attacked.

Jake stared in amazement as the *Divine Wind* lunged towards the three ships, its front cannon targeting the *Black Death*. Had he really expected anything less of Crazy Kay Jagger? The *Black Death* took several hits before it shifted into gear and returned fire. It sprayed the *Divine Wind* with red laser bolts, like a shower of blood, but the star frigate's patched-up shields held together.

Kay was the toughest teenager that Jake had ever met, but her ship didn't stand a chance on its own.

'What are you waiting for, Nichelle?' asked Granny Leatherhead.

'Aye, captain.'

Jake had expected the Space Dogs to turn and run, as they had done previously. But instead, the old cargo hauler powered towards the *Black Death*.

'This is for Wild Joe Jagger,' said Granny Leatherhead. 'Kodan, introduce that metal-mouthed murderer to Old Lizzy.'

A string of laser bolts burst from the nose of the cargo hauler and struck the shields of the *Black Death*.

'Watch out,' warned Farid.

Carla Gritt joined the battle, pulling in front of them and unloading her laser cannon. Nichelle swerved to avoid the space cutter, forcing Kodan to break off his attack.

'That flaming fortune seeker,' fumed Granny Leatherhead. 'Take her out so we can get back to Scarabus.'

'What about the *Lost Soul*?' asked Nichelle.

'Ignore it,' said Granny Leatherhead. 'We'll deal with James Hawker later.'

The *Dark Horse* tore after the *Loose Cannon*, chipping away at its shields, trying to get a clear shot.

Jake's insides turned as the ship dipped and weaved. He kept the rear laser cannon pointed at the *Lost Soul* in case it tried to creep up behind them, but the large black cruiser remained in position with its gun ports closed. Why was it holding back? What was it waiting for?

The *Divine Wind* soared over his head with a large section of hull missing, where the *Black Death* had blasted through its shields. Jake watched the huge warship storm after the damaged star frigate and knew that he was the only one who could help. He gripped the rubber handlebars and swung the laser cannon around, catching the *Black Death* in his sights.

'Leave them alone, you wretchard.'

Jake pulled the trigger and held on as the cannon fired. His laser bolts caught the side of the pirate warship, but they failed to penetrate its shields. He fired again, targeting its weak spots, such as the gun ports and exhausts. To his surprise, most of his shots were on target. It was probably because the *Black Death* was a lot bigger and slower than the Gork fighter craft. Whatever the reason, it encouraged him to keep up the attack.

Desperate to help Kay and her crew, Jake continued to fire short bursts, taking care not to overheat the weapon. His shots must have caused some damage to the *Black Death*, because the warship broke off its pursuit and came after the *Dark Horse* instead. Jake took one look at the blood-streaked hull and suddenly felt exposed in his little turret. He fired another burst from his laser cannon and hoped that the rest of the crew had noticed what was happening.

A barrage of red laser bolts struck the *Dark Horse* from behind. The *Black Death* was so close now that Jake could make out Scarabus Shark standing on its bridge. He fired a couple of shots at the oily-skinned captain, but they bounced off the shields. A large panel opened below the bridge window like a gaping mouth in the warship's hull. At first, Jake feared that the *Black Death* had a multi-barrelled laser cannon like Old Lizzy, but its contents were much worse. A circle of fire glowed deep inside and something burst out of the hole.

'Torpedo!' he shouted, but no one could hear him.

The huge red missile headed straight for them. In a moment of panic, Jake did the only thing that made any sense. He aimed his laser cannon at the torpedo and pulled the trigger.

Boom!

It may have been luck, or the sheer number of laser bolts that Jake fired, but the torpedo exploded in open space, causing both the *Dark Horse* and the *Black Death* to veer in opposite directions. Jake was thrown from his saddle as the blast hit. He flew into the air and crashed into the dome roof with such force, he was amazed that the glass didn't break.

'What the fluff was that?' said Granny Leatherhead, as the cargo hauler creaked and shuddered to a halt.

'We've been hit,' reported Farid. 'An explosion has knocked out our shields and exhausts.'

'The ship is not responding,' said Nichelle. 'I've lost control.'

Jake looked outside and saw bits of jagged metal where the exhausts had been. It was a miracle that his turret had only suffered a few scratches on its smudged glass. With a great effort, he climbed back on to his laser cannon and listened eagerly to the intercom.

'What happened to the *Black Death*?' asked Granny Leatherhead.

'It's damaged,' said Farid. 'But still operational.'

Jake tried to block out the pain as he scanned the stars. He spotted the pirate warship circling back around to finish them. Its shields were down and its hull was buckled, but it looked in a better shape than the *Dark Horse*. As it lined up to attack, Jake took aim and fired, but a single laser cannon was no match for the *Black*

Death. It flew towards them, weapons blazing. Scarabus Shark had the old cargo hauler firmly in his sights and there was nothing Jake could do to stop him.

'Crash!'

The *Divine Wind* hurtled into view and rammed the *Black Death*, sending both ships spinning off at angles with bits of debris flying in all directions. Jake watched the star frigate cartwheel through space, its yellow hull mashed and its exhausts crumpled, while the *Black Death* tumbled off course away from the *Dark Horse*.

'Madness,' muttered Granny Leatherhead.

The *Divine Wind* stopped turning and became motionless. Jake wondered if Kay was all right, or if she had been hurt in the collision. His eyes scanned her ship, trying to detect signs of life.

'Ahoy, *Divine Wind*,' hailed Farid. 'Are you there, Kay?'

Jake pressed his ears to the intercom speaker. At first there was only static, but then a weak and husky voice responded.

'Ahoy-hoy,' wheezed Kay. 'We're still here, mates, but the ship is a total wreck.'

'Can you fix it?' asked Granny Leatherhead.

'We might be able to do something with the engine, if we had a couple of hours.'

Jake knew that they didn't have a couple of minutes, because despite everything, the *Black Death* still had power. It turned slowly towards the *Divine Wind* and Scarabus Shark's voice rasped through the speaker.

'You put up a good fight, Kay,' he said. 'But you've got nothing left. It's time to join your daddy.'

Chapter 20

Rusty's Revenge

'No!' cried Jake.

In a fit of panic, he fired the laser cannon at the *Black Death*, no longer caring if it overheated, but it wasn't enough to stop the old warship. The *Black Death* stopped in front of the *Divine Wind*, like an executioner towering over the condemned. Jake's eyes scanned the crumpled crimson hull and spotted a large crack near the rear, where he knew the engine room was located. If there was an engine, there would be fuel cells.

Without hesitation, Jake swung his cannon and fired. His first two shots grazed the hull, but the third flew straight into the crack and disappeared. For a moment, nothing happened, and then the *Black Death* exploded from the inside, blowing itself apart in a series of blinding flashes. Jake braced himself as the shock-waves hit the *Dark Horse*, followed by shards of metal.

'Good shot, Kid Cutler,' cackled Granny Leatherhead over the intercom.

Jake could hear Farid and Nichelle cheering in the background, but their celebration was short-lived. Two ships remained: the *Lost Soul* and the *Loose Cannon*.

'Thanks, Jake,' said Kay, her husky voice filling the turret. 'We're stuffed now, but at least we took that wretchard with us.'

The *Loose Cannon* circled the two ships, steering clear of Old Lizzy and the sawn-off laser cannon. Jake spotted a long hose dangling from its hull and knew that Carla Gritt was preparing to give them another acid shower. He fired several shots in her direction before his cannon finally overheated.

'What do we do now, captain?' asked Nichelle.

'What can we do?' said Granny Leatherhead. 'Without exhausts, we're an easy target.'

In the distance, the *Lost Soul* stirred and moved towards them, its gun ports open and its laser cannon primed. If the acid shower didn't destroy them, James Hawker would finish them off.

'Hey, it was fun while it lasted,' said Kay. 'At least I got to meet the infamous Jake Cutler.'

Jake sat back from his laser cannon. Why did it have to end like this? If only he could speak to Kay and thank her for everything she had done for them. He thought about Kella, Nanoo and the Space Dogs.

They had been through so much together and now Jake was going to die alone in his turret.

What about his father? He would never find out what had happened to Andras Cutler. As for saving the independent colonies, it would now be up to Hector Rumpole to prevent a galactic war. Jake was sickened to think that millions might die so James Hawker and Carla Gritt could collect a reward.

'Captain, I've picked up another ship on the scanners,' said Farid.

'I wondered when the Interstellar Navy would show up,' she croaked.

'It's not naval. In fact, there are no signs of life aboard. If it wasn't moving so fast, I would have dismissed it as a wreck.'

'What are you saying? We've got an incoming ghost ship?'

'Not ghosts,' he said. 'Robots.'

Jake glanced up to see *Rusty's Revenge* soar into view. The pirate ship had been converted from a space tug with armour plating and a battering ram. It opened fire, its front weapons tearing holes in the *Loose Cannon*. Carla Gritt took evasive action, but her ship stumbled into the path of the cargo hauler's sawn-off laser cannon. Maaka and Woorak blasted the side of the *Loose Cannon*, while the Hacker Jackers continued their overhead assault. Even the *Divine Wind* managed to get a few shots in with its last remaining weapon.

It was too much for the old space cutter. A laser bolt penetrated its hull and ruptured the acid tank, flooding the ship with corrosive fluid. Jake watched as the *Loose Cannon* disintegrated before their eyes.

'Captain, should we let space have her?' asked Maaka over the intercom.

'Are you pulling my pistols?' barked Granny Leatherhead. 'Keep firing. I'm not taking any chances this time.'

Within seconds, the *Loose Cannon* was reduced to stardust. It was now three pirate ships against one and Jake's laser cannon had almost cooled down. *Rusty's Revenge* positioned itself between the *Dark Horse* and the *Divine Wind*, so all three craft faced the *Lost Soul*.

'Come on!' shouted Jake at the black cruiser. 'What are you waiting for?'

The *Lost Soul* lingered for a moment, like a spider waiting to pounce. But instead of attacking, it turned and fled. Jake slipped off his saddle in surprise. He had expected fearless James Hawker to put up more of a fight.

'Captain, the Starbucklers are making a run for it,' said Farid. 'It's over, we've won.'

A cheer exploded through the ship's intercom as the crew celebrated.

'Magnifty,' cried Jake, punching the air. 'Mag-flipping-nifty.'

The Space Dogs and the Luna Ticks had done it – they had beaten the top two spacejackers in the galaxy and a ruthless fortune seeker. Jake felt incredible, as though he could take on the whole Interstellar Navy on his own. He joined in the cheering, making himself hoarse, until a familiar electronic voice made contact.

'Ahoy, Captains Leatherhead and Jagger,' said Vigor-8. 'Can we assist you?'

'Ahoy, Captain 8,' croaked Granny Leatherhead. 'It's good to see you and your courageous crew of robot raiders. I don't suppose you have any mainte-nance droids on board your ship?'

It took the Hacker Jackers an hour to patch up the *Dark Horse* and *Divine Wind*, but the two ships were still vulnerable. Vigor-8 took Jake aboard *Rusty's Revenge* and introduced him to the crew of free robots. Jake thanked each one in turn for their help, before the robot captain escorted him back to the *Dark Horse*.

'You helped me in Papa Don's and showed me respect,' said Vigor-8. 'Now I have returned the favour.'

'It wasn't just our crews you saved today,' said Jake. 'If I can prevent a galactic war, the entire seven solar systems will owe the Hacker Jackers.'

Vigor-8 stopped and tilted its head. 'I don't understand.'

Jake explained about the Interstellar Government's plans to wipe out the independent colonies.

'Is that why you need Papa Don's sword?' asked Vigor-8.

'Yes,' said Jake. 'It will help me to convince the independent colony leaders that I'm telling the truth.'

'Do people often not believe you?'

Jake laughed. 'Only when I talk about Altus.'

'Altus?' Vigor-8 paused. 'You are a most unusual spacejacker, Jake Cutler.'

The airlock door opened and they entered the *Dark Horse*. Jake took Vigor-8 up to the bridge to say goodbye to Granny Leatherhead.

'Thanks again, Captain 8,' said the captain. 'It's good to know that we have friends out here in space.'

Vigor-8 held its chest and bowed. 'You're most welcome, Captain Leatherhead.'

'I wonder –'

'Captain,' interrupted Farid. 'I've picked up three naval warships on the long-range scanner and they're heading straight for us.'

Granny Leatherhead glanced at her damaged ship. 'Captain 8, could you do me another favour?'

Vigor-8 snapped to attention and saluted. 'Name it.'

'Jake needs a lift to Santanova in the fourth solar system,' she said. 'Can you take him?'

'Yes.'

Jake tried to protest, but Granny Leatherhead refused to listen. 'I'm sorry, Kid Cutler, but even if the *Dark Horse* could make it to the gathering on time, the Space Dogs would never get past the security. *Rusty's Revenge* stands a much better chance of getting you there in one piece.'

'What about Kella and Nanoo?'

'You should take them with you. A lilac-skinned alien and a United Worlds crystal healer might help to back up your story. But I would leave Kay behind, in case she decides to do something crazy in the middle of your speech.'

'What will you do?' asked Jake. 'Where will you go?'

'No idea,' said Granny Leatherhead. 'We'll start by leaving a false trail for the Interstellar Navy to follow and then stop somewhere for repairs. Now hurry up and go, before that adamant admiral gets here.'

Jake paused in the doorway. 'How will I find you?'

'Don't worry, we'll show up when the time is right.'

Vigor-8 helped Jake to collect his things from the guest quarters, including his Altian uniform, his hand-held computer, his scribbled speech notes and the sword of Altus. By the time they returned to the airlock, most of the crew had gathered there to see them off. A moment later, Kella and Nanoo hurried up the corridor with their bags.

'I'll understand if you two want to stay aboard the *Dark Horse*,' said Jake.

'And miss fun?' joked Nanoo. 'I want to be at historic event with my friend, before I return to Taan-Centaur.'

'What about you, Kella?'

'I want to help you to unite the independent colonies and stop the Interstellar Navy,' she said. 'It's what Jeyne would have done. I may not be able to save my sister, but at least I can make a stand on her behalf.'

Jake nodded and smiled.

'Come on, you lot,' croaked Granny Leatherhead. 'You've got a gathering to catch.'

'Thanks for everything, captain,' he said, picking up his bag.

'Have you got your speech?'

'Right here.' Jake patted his pocket. 'I hope it's enough to convince the other leaders.'

'You'll be fine,' she said. 'You've stood up to me enough times.'

Scargus stepped forward with something wrapped inside a blanket. 'Don't forget your crown.'

Jake had hoped to sneak off without the metal monstrosity. He made a mental note to leave it on *Rusty's Revenge* when they reached Santanova. With a dramatic flick of his wrist, the chief engineer whipped off the blanket to reveal the finished result.

'What do you think?' asked Scargus.

Jake couldn't believe it was the same pile of junk. It was … beautiful.

'It's magnifty,' he said. 'A work of art.'

Scargus beamed. 'I smoothed the edges and sprayed it gold before rubbing it in engine oil and boot polish to make it look old.'

'Where did you get the fur trimming?' asked Jake, taking the crown and examining it.

Scargus looked embarrassed and pointed at his bushy beard, which was a lot shorter than usual.

'Come on, we don't have much time,' said Granny Leatherhead. 'This whole area is going to be flooded with naval warships.'

Jake, Kella and Nanoo said their goodbyes and followed Vigor-8 aboard *Rusty's Revenge*. It felt strange to leave the Space Dogs after everything they had been through together. Jake turned to catch a final glimpse of his shipmates as the airlock door shut. Why did everything have to end with a closing door? If he ever returned to Altus, he vowed to remove the doors in his mansion, so people could come and go when they pleased.

As the three of them left the airlock and entered the converted space tug, Nanoo passed a small bundle to Jake.

'I make something for you to wear at gathering,' he said. 'It what I've been working on in engine room.'

Jake unfolded a strange-looking blue waistcoat, which could have easily been made by a toddler using wrapping paper. It wafted weightlessly in the zero gravity, while rows of little blue squares shimmered in the light. Kella looked as though she was supressing a laugh.

'It's very … unique,' said Jake, hoping that he wasn't expected to wear it in front of the other leaders.

Nanoo pointed at the untidy stitching. 'It not easy to make and I not good at sewing.'

'No kidding,' said Jake. 'That's kind of you, mate, but I already have something to wear at the gathering.'

'Yes, I know, this vest go under uniform,' explained Nanoo.

'It looks a bit scratchy for a vest,' commented Kella.

'Not any vest,' said Nanoo. 'It a laserproof vest.'

'No way.' Jake was suddenly a lot more interested in the waistcoat. 'You made me a laserproof vest?'

'It deflect laser from pistol and rifle, but not cannon,' said Nanoo.

'You're a genius.' Jake held it up against his body. 'But what makes you think I need protection?'

Nanoo shrugged. 'Maybe some leaders want to have war with United Worlds.'

Kella eyed the vest curiously. 'What if they shoot him in the head?'

It took *Rusty's Revenge* less than two days to reach Santanova. The Hacker Jackers were not as wanted as the Space Dogs, meaning that they could take a more direct route while still avoiding the Interstellar Navy. Jake had spent the voyage finishing his speech and talking with the crew. Nanoo had even managed to fix some of their damaged parts.

There had not been much food aboard the ship, unless you counted spare batteries and engine oil. Kella had packed a few space biscuits in her bag, which had kept them going the first day. However, by the time *Rusty's Revenge* reached the fourth solar system, the three of them were ravenous.

A couple of ex-house robots had constructed beds for them, but they were hard and uncomfortable. Jake had found it impossible to sleep while worrying about the gathering. His mind often wandered to Callidus, Capio and the Space Dogs. What would happen to them if war broke out?

Santanova was the largest and wealthiest independent colony in the galaxy. It had even more crystals than Reus in the seventh solar system. Altus was a lot smaller than both of these planets, but its three crystal moons meant that it was worth more than Santanova and Reus put together. Jake wondered how the prime minister of Santanova would react when she found out that Altus was real.

As they entered the fourth solar system, Jake, Kella and Nanoo were summoned to the bridge.

Vigor-8 stood by the front window, bathed in light from the huge red sun, which glinted off its chipped chest plate like flecks of blood. A few ex-house robots scurried around the room while a multi-limbed maintenance droid piloted the ship. Jake spotted a planet covered in yellow and orange swirls, orbited by a single black moon.

'Santanova,' announced Vigor-8. 'One of the oldest and most respected independent colonies in the seven solar systems.'

'It huge,' said Nanoo. 'I never see such a big world.'

'How will we get past the planetary guard?' asked Jake, noticing clusters of fighter craft in a low orbit.

The United Worlds were not welcome at the gathering and the Interstellar Navy would be kept out at all costs.

'This is as far as we can take you,' said Vigor-8. 'There is too much security for us to land on the surface.'

'How will we get to the gathering?' asked Jake.

'Escape pod.'

'Pardon?'

'There are two escape pods aboard this ship,' said Vigor-8. 'You can have one of them. It will be programmed to land in the space docks outside Lugar. From there, you can catch a hover-train into the city.'

'But we don't have any money,' said Kella.

Vigor-8 stalked over to a large chest at the rear of the bridge and flipped it open. Inside was enough gold and jewels to make Granny Leatherhead's eye pop out. The robot captain rammed its hand inside the chest and pulled out a fistful of crystals.

'Is this sufficient?'

All three of them nodded. It was probably enough to hire the whole train.

Chapter 21

Santanova

Jake, Kella and Nanoo collected their things and met Vigor-8 by a circular hatch on the side of the ship. The robot captain opened it to reveal a small capsule with padded walls and a porthole window.

'Thanks again,' said Jake, holding out his hand. 'We owe you our lives.'

Vigor-8 took the hand and squeezed it with cold metal fingers. 'Good luck, Jake Cutler.'

The three of them stepped inside the escape pod and secured their straps. Jake glanced out of the window and saw a stream of spacecraft heading to Santanova. His eyes scanned the planet surface until he found the largest city, Lugar, where he would deliver his speech. It looked a long way down.

Vigor-8 sealed the hatch and activated the launch sequence. Jake, Kella and Nanoo checked their straps and braced themselves. A second later, docking clamps released and the escape pod fired into space like a spinning cannonball. Jake was thrown back in his seat as they hurtled towards the planet surface. His body grew heavier with the effects of gravity and wisps of atmosphere licked the window.

'How we steer this thing?' asked Nanoo.

'We don't,' said Jake. 'It's programmed to land in the space docks.'

'Is it me, or is it getting hot in here?' asked Kella.

'That because we entering planet atmosphere,' said Nanoo. 'You not normally feel it, because ship hulls are thicker.'

The escape pod tore into clear skies and the temperature dropped. A small blue light flashed and short bursts of thrust slowed their descent. Jake caught sight of the busy space docks below. He hoped that the Hacker Jackers had picked a quiet spot for them to land.

'Here we go,' he said. 'Hold on tight.'

Jake felt the thruster jets fire in full, but the escape pod was still falling fast. The space docks seemed to rise up to meet them until ... crash! Jake, Kella and Nanoo were thrown about in their seats as the capsule hit the ground and rolled thirty metres before colliding with the outer dock wall.

Jake hung upside down in his seat, his body bruised and his head spinning. Kella and Nanoo moaned with pain as they crawled from the battered escape pod. Jake joined them and saw that they had touched down behind one of the largest docking terminals. He doubted their arrival had been unnoticed.

'Let's move,' he said. 'Before someone discovers the escape pod.'

The space docks were by far the cleanest that Jake had ever visited. How grubby *Rusty's Revenge* would have looked next to the more luxurious vessels. Jake reached into his bag and pulled out Maaka's sunglasses, which he had borrowed to conceal his purple eye implants.

'I can't believe that we're actually here,' said Kella. 'I've always wanted to see Santanova.'

Nanoo rubbed his stomach. 'Let us get food.'

The three of them made their way to the main terminal, where they used their crystals to buy stellar-burgers. There were no smugglers or pirates in the space docks, only crowds of independent colonists from across the seven solar systems. Jake even spotted a couple of cyber-monks in grey hooded robes. The atmosphere felt warm and friendly, like a festival.

Nanoo attracted a few odd looks because of his lilac skin, but he didn't seem to mind. All three of them were just glad to be somewhere with real food and fresh air. A man with a heavily scarred face almost tripped over when he saw them. Jake wondered if people could tell they were space pirates.

'We should book transport to Lugar,' suggested Kella.

'Good idea,' said Jake. 'And get a hotel room. I could do with a shower and some sleep before the gathering.'

Jake wanted to look his best in case his father was watching the *Interstellar News*. He also wanted somewhere quiet to send Hector Rumpole an e-comm.

'Where we meet Callidus and Capio?' asked Nanoo.

'I don't know,' said Jake. 'I've not heard anything since they visited the asteroid miners.'

Kella purchased three hover-train tickets to Lugar the next morning. It cost her half of the crystals to get a private compartment, but it was worth it, as most of the carriages were now fully booked. Kella then took Nanoo shopping for new clothes, so they didn't look out of place when Jake put on his uniform.

Jake waited for them in the hotel room. He used his handheld computer to send Hector Rumpole an e-comm, letting him know that they had arrived safely. After that, Jake lay on the soft bed to watch the *Interstellar News*. There were several shots of Santanova and a chamber full of seats. A reporter explained that this was where the gathering would be held the next morning. In front of each seat rested a small sign containing the name of a leader and their independent colony. The camera paused by a lone seat at the front of the room, which was reserved for the *Ruler of Altus*.

'It's good to know that the mayor of Remota has a sense of humour,' said the reporter. 'Let's hope the other leaders see the funny side tomorrow.'

Jake groaned and turned off the display screen. Would people take him seriously when he took that seat in the morning? What if everyone laughed? At least there had been no mention of the Space Dogs or Luna Ticks on the *Interstellar News*, which hopefully meant that they had evaded the naval warships.

With a great effort, Jake forced himself off the bed and into the bathroom to freshen up. It turned out to be the best shower he had taken since leaving Altus. He lingered under the hot water, sampling every gel and lotion provided. How different it was to the mouldy washrooms in the monastery where he had grown up.

Had it only been four months since he'd left Remota? It seemed like a lifetime ago. All of those years studying in the tech-library and sketching ships in the space docks were now distant memories. He was no longer the same innocent boy who had once dreamt of adventures in space. His eyes had been opened to a vast and dangerous universe.

When he eventually turned off the shower, Jake heard an impatient buzzing sound. Was that the door? He wrapped a towel around his waist and rushed across the hotel room, but by the time he reached the videocom, the caller had gone. Jake spotted a piece of folded paper tucked under the door. It was a note addressed to him. He scooped it up and read it:

I have news about your father. Meet me at ten o'clock tomorrow morning in the main restaurant. I'll be sitting at table six near the window. Come alone. JD.

Water dripped on the floor as Jake read the note twice more, his hands trembling with excitement. Who was JD and how did they know that he was staying in the space docks? If there was the slightest chance that this person had news about his father, then he wanted to meet them.

Jake dried himself and slipped on a hotel robe. He paced the room with the note clutched in his hand. What did it mean? Would the news be good or bad? Jake would have to wait until the morning to find out. If only he hadn't been in the shower when

JD had called. He glanced at a clock on the display screen and sighed.

The videocom buzzed and Jake jumped in surprise. Had JD returned? He scrambled to open the door, his pulse racing.

'Hello,' said Nanoo, standing in the corridor laden with shopping bags.

'What's that smell?' asked Kella. 'Are you wearing aftershave?'

Jake tried not to look disappointed to see his friends.

Nanoo entered and whistled. 'It nice room. I like big bed.'

Kella and Nanoo dumped their bags while Jake checked the empty corridor and closed the door.

'We've bought new outfits,' said Kella. 'I can't wait to get out of these old clothes.'

'We also bring food.' Nanoo pointed to a couple of takeaway cartons sticking out of one bag. 'Kella, tell Jake about security.'

'Oh yeah, there are planetary guards everywhere. It's not going to be easy to catch the hover-train in the morning.'

'It'll be fine,' muttered Jake, distracted.

Kella raised her eyebrows. 'You're the infamous Jake Cutler, notorious purple-eyed space pirate. How do you propose we sneak you and your golden cutlass past security? Not to mention a Novu alien and a United World citizen.'

'Hector Rumpole will sort it. I sent him an e-comm.'

'How can you be sure?'

'You OK, mate?' asked Nanoo.

Jake looked at them for a moment and then held up the piece of paper.

'I received this note,' he said, handing it to them.

Kella read the message.

'Is this for real?' she asked. 'Who is JD?'

'No idea,' said Jake. 'I don't know anyone with those initials.'

'What about that farmer on Altus?' she suggested.

'John Daxton?' Jake recalled a timid man with a tall straw hat. 'What would he be doing here?'

Kella shrugged.

'This could be trap,' said Nanoo. 'How you know it safe?'

Jake could not answer. There was no way of knowing if the note was genuine or a fortune seeker trick, but it was a risk that he was willing to take to find his father.

Kella read the note again. 'It says ten o'clock tomorrow morning, but your speech is at nine in Lugar.'

'I know,' said Jake. 'What am I going to do?'

Kella frowned at him. 'You have to be at the gathering. Who else can unite the independent colonies?'

Jake snatched back the note. 'But this JD might know where to find my dad. I may never get a chance like this again.'

'There is not choice,' said Nanoo. 'You must prevent galactic war.'

Jake stared longingly at the piece of paper in his hand, but he knew they were right. It didn't matter how much he wanted to meet JD, there was nothing more important than stopping the Interstellar Navy.

'OK,' he said, folding the note and tucking it into his pocket. 'I'll do my duty.'

Jake climbed on to the bed to watch the *Interstellar News* while Kella and Nanoo busied themselves with the takeaway. After they had eaten, Kella showered and Nanoo hung up his new clothes. Jake remained on the bed, nursing a bottle of apple juice. He couldn't stop thinking about his father. If only there was a way to be at the gathering and meet JD.

'You not practice speech?' asked Nanoo.

'Hmm?' said Jake. 'Oh, yeah, I'll rehearse it later.'

Kella came out of the bathroom in a cloud of steam, wearing hotel pyjamas. Her hair was wrapped in a towel and her cheeks were pink from the heat.

'That felt so good,' she said. 'I've washed half of the galaxy out of my hair.'

Jake smiled. 'I'd forgotten what you looked like under all that dirt.'

Kella ignored him and perched on the edge of the bed. 'Anything in the news?'

Jake hadn't really been paying attention. He quickly read the scrolling headline on the display screen.

'The independent colony leaders are arriving in Lugar city ahead of the gathering.'

'Do you recognise any of them?' she asked.

'I doubt it.' Jake had never been that interested in galactic politics, though he had seen the president of Reus on the stellar-net a few times.

'At least they're smiling and waving,' she said.

Jake spotted a man with a bulbous nose and ruddy cheeks. 'Hey, that's the mayor of Remota.'

'You mean the one who looking worried?' asked Nanoo.

Hector Rumpole did appear anxious as he stroked his walrus moustache. It must have taken a lot to sort out the gathering at short notice. If the plan failed, he would be held responsible. Jake suddenly appreciated how much the mayor was doing for him. Not many people would organise a major conference on the word of a thirteen-year-old space pirate.

'We should get some rest,' said Kella. 'It's going to be a big day tomorrow.'

Chapter 22

The Gathering

It was several hours later when Jake woke with a start. His first thought was that they had overslept. He sat up and checked the clock on the display screen, but it was still early. Kella and Nanoo were fast asleep either side of him.

Jake lay back down and thought about the note from JD. If the stranger had nothing to hide, why ask him to come alone? On the other hand, if it was a trap, why meet in the main restaurant? Jake figured that JD would explain everything when they met, except they weren't going to meet. Not unless there was a way for Jake to stay in the space docks and make his speech in Lugar city.

Unable to sleep, Jake crawled out of bed and checked his handheld computer. Hector Rumpole had replied to the e-comm, but his response was short:

Jake. I'm glad you arrived safely. Meet me at the Chamber of Parliament tomorrow morning before nine o'clock. Hector.

Jake turned off the device and crept into the bathroom to change into his Altian uniform. He took care not to rattle the various buttons and buckles as he dressed. It was still hours until the gathering, but he wanted to be ready for the day ahead. When he finished, he transferred JD's note to his jacket pocket and spent the next hour rehearsing his speech in front of the mirror.

Jake was hungry by the time Kella and Nanoo stirred. The three of them ate leftover takeaway for breakfast before packing their bags and leaving to catch the hover-train. As expected, the space docks swarmed with planetary guards, who wore smart orange armour and carried long laser rifles. There were also a number of checkpoints, where people were forced to walk through security scanners.

Jake covered his purple eyes with Maaka's sunglasses and hid the sword of Altus inside his laser-proof vest. If the little blue squares could deflect lasers, perhaps they would stop the security scanners as well. Kella and Nanoo wore space helmets with tinted visors, so their faces could not be seen clearly. Nanoo also wore a scarf and gloves to conceal his lilac skin.

After passing through several checkpoints unchallenged, the three of them reached the hover-train platform. It was heavily crowded, which made it easier to hide from the planetary guards. Jake checked that the fake crown was still tucked safely in his bag. The red morning sky was full of spacecraft waiting to land, but there was no sign of the *Dark Horse* or *Divine Wind*.

'Here come train,' said Nanoo, pointing to a hole in the space-dock walls.

Jake heard a powerful engine and felt a rush of hot air. A large silver hover-train slid into view and pulled up alongside the platform. Its brakes emitted great plumes of steam as they hissed and creaked. The crowd surged forward as people rushed to find their carriages. Jake, Kella and Nanoo fought their way to the rear of the train, where they had reserved a private compartment. It meant that Kella and Nanoo could take off their helmets, while Jake could remove his sunglasses, without fear of being spotted.

'Not bad,' said Kella, as they closed the door. 'I could get used to Santanova.'

Nanoo's wide turquoise eyes explored the modern compartment interior. 'It like the trains on Taan-Centaur.'

The hover-train left the platform and accelerated out of the space docks. It glided smoothly across the Santanovan landscape like a long silver snake, weaving between farms and factories. Jake watched through the window as they approached Lugar a short distance away. He knew it was the largest of the independent colony cities, but nothing had prepared him for the mass of towering skyscrapers, which stretched into the air like a wall of concrete and glass. It made him realise that he was trying to save a galaxy that he hardly knew. He hoped that he would get the chance to explore it properly one day.

The hover-train reached the edge of the city and disappeared into a dark underground tunnel. It rumbled noisily beneath the surface for several minutes before emerging inside Lugar Central Station. Jake spotted planetary guards lining the platform and signalled for Kella and Nanoo to don their helmets. If they were lucky, they could blend in with the crowd and slip by unnoticed.

When the hover-train doors opened, the three of them stepped on to the platform behind a family of four. Jake risked a glance at the planetary guards, who stood watching the passengers. In front of him, two guards had stopped the family and were asking for their identification. Jake carried on walking while the guards were distracted.

'Hey, look, that boy has purple eyes,' said a young girl.

Jake turned in surprise to see her pointing at him. His fingers reached for his face and he realised that he wasn't wearing Maaka's sunglasses. He sheilded his eyes with his hand and hurried towards the exit, but it was too late.

'Halt,' ordered one of the guards.

'Stop him,' shouted another.

Several planetary guards blocked the exit, while others pushed their way through the crowd.

'What do we do?' hissed Kella.

Jake twisted on the spot, trying to locate another way out, but they were surrounded. He placed a hand on his sword as the crowd parted and an officer stepped forward.

'Are you Jake Cutler?'

'That's right.' It seemed pointless to pretend otherwise.

'Good, we've been expecting you.'

'You have?' asked Jake.

'Yes, we have a hover-car waiting outside,' said the officer. 'The mayor of Remota will meet you at the Chamber of Parliament.'

'Ah, there you are,' said Hector Rumpole jovially. 'I was starting to worry that you weren't coming.'

The ruddy-cheeked mayor had been waiting for them on a set of steps outside the huge parliament building. He wore a warm smile beneath his bushy moustache, which did not match his tired eyes. The streets were full of people and the air buzzed with camera drones. Images of the inside chamber were broadcast on outdoor display screens.

'It's good to see you again, Mayor Rumpole,' said Jake. 'These are my friends, Kella and Nanoo. Kella is a crystal healer and Nanoo is a Novu alien from a distant galaxy.'

'Great gubbins!' Hector Rumpole caught sight of Nanoo's lilac skin. 'You do keep interesting company. It's a pleasure to meet you both, but we must hurry. The leaders have started to gather in the grand chamber. You can wait in another room while I introduce you.'

Jake's maroon uniform was attracting attention from the crowd, even if they didn't recognise the emblem on his chest. It was funny to think that within a few hours, everyone in the galaxy would know it was the symbol of Altus. Hector Rumpole waved to the cameras and escorted the three of them into the building. Inside the huge entrance doors, old portraits lined the walls and four words decorated the floor: *United in our independence*.

'What that mean?' asked Nanoo.

'It means that we have a chance,' said Jake.

The mayor led them down a busy corridor to a small black door. He stopped outside and checked that the coast was clear.

'Do you have your speech?' he asked.

'Yes,' said Jake, pulling the scribbled notes from his pocket. 'I've memorised every word.'

'Good, very good.' Hector Rumpole opened the small door. 'Wait in here until you're summoned. We start in ten minutes. Best of luck, Jake.'

The three of them entered a small room with no windows. A few chairs surrounded a narrow glass table, on which rested bottles of water. At the opposite end of the room were two huge mahogany doors. Jake could hear voices on the other side and assumed it was the grand chamber. He pulled the fake crown from his bag and waited for the gathering to start. When he had imagined this moment, he had been relaxed and confident, but now it felt suddenly real and daunting.

The minutes crept by and before Jake knew it, the chamber echoed with ceremonial music. When it faded, Hector Rumpole started talking, but Jake was only half listening. All he could think about was how soon he would have to deliver his own speech. Was he ready? He had practised the words a hundred times, but somehow it didn't seem enough. Jake closed his eyes and took a deep breath. Nerves were a luxury that he could no longer afford.

Hector Rumpole's voice grew louder and some of his words caught Jake's attention. 'A special young man ... an incredible adventure ... an important message ...'

The huge mahogany doors cracked open and an elderly steward entered the room. 'Are you ready, my lord?'

It was time. The entire galaxy was waiting for the ruler of Altus. No more worrying about the speech or if he was ready to deliver it: the moment he had been planning had arrived. Jake straightened his uniform and checked his reflection in the handheld computer screen. With trembling hands, he placed the fake crown on his head and drew the sword of Altus.

'My lord?' pressed the steward, holding open the door.

'I'm ready,' said Jake, his heart pounding.

With a final glance at Kella and Nanoo, he stepped through the door. The bright lights and scattered applause reminded Jake of the Reus roulette arena in Papa Don's. He recalled how confident Kodan had appeared at that moment. It made him realise the importance of a strong first impression. Jake lifted his head and entered the grand chamber.

The doorway led into a vast circular room with dark wooden beams and a muralled ceiling. There were more people than he had expected crammed into the rows of seats. It seemed that each of the leaders had brought a number of advisers with them. A flock of camera drones flitted around the chamber, recording the historic event. Jake glanced at their twitching lenses and tried not to think how many people were watching.

Hector Rumpole stood at the front of the room, next to the seat reserved for the ruler of Altus. Jake checked his pocket as he walked over to the mayor. He had memorised his speech, but it was reassuring to know that his notes were there if needed. His hand touched something else, the message from JD, and for a moment he was distracted.

'Jake?' whispered Hector Rumpole, holding out a microphone. 'The galaxy is waiting.'

Jake turned to look at the wall of curious faces, many of which were obscured behind the bright lights. He could sense their scepticism, but he had expected nothing less.

Jake took the microphone from Hector Rumpole, but he did not sit down. If he was going to make a stand, it seemed appropriate to do it on his feet.

'My fellow leaders, my name is Jake Cutler and I am the ruler of Altus.'

It was strange to hear his own voice amplified through powerful speakers. He paused while people muttered and laughed.

'I bring you grave news and tidings of war,' he said, and the laughter stopped. 'Altus does exist. I know this will be hard for you to accept, but I have proof. This uniform, this pendant around my neck, this golden cutlass ...'

Jake hesitated at the crown. If he wanted people to trust him, he was not going to lie. His hand slipped away from his head.

'These are unique items from my home planet. Altus has remained hidden for centuries and I am betraying its people by speaking here today, but what I have to say is important. If nothing else, Altus is a symbol of independence, the idea that a planet can survive in isolation, cut off from the wider universe.'

Jake glanced at Hector Rumpole, who smiled encouragingly.

'There have always been independent colonies in the seven solar systems, long before the United Worlds were formed. For hundreds of years, we have retained our independence, even in the most challenging of times. We're proud to be our own masters, but we also respect and celebrate our differences. This is something that we have in common. It has defined who we are and what we stand for. In many ways, it unites us.'

To Jake's surprise, a few people clapped.

'I cannot reveal to you the location of Altus today, not while the Galactic Trade Corporation is hunting its three crystal moons. However, I look forward to the day when the Altian people can come out of hiding and stand proud alongside the other colonies. But we cannot take our independence for granted. My space pirate friends and I have learnt of a plot to wipe out our colonies forever.'

This statement was greeted with a ripple of angry murmurs. Jake refused to pause and pushed on, talking louder into the microphone.

'The Interstellar Navy is using the Gorks to strengthen its fleet. Admiral Vantard has dispatched naval warships to the seventh solar system to start a galactic war. This threat is real. The freedom of our planets and the lives of our people are at stake. If we do not act now, Vantos will be attacked within hours, followed by Abbere and Torbana. The independent colonies will fall, one solar system at a time, until there are not enough of us left to fight back.'

Several people stood up and shook their fists, but their rage was not directed at Jake. He read their signs and realised that they were the leaders from Vantos, Abbere and Torbana, who had left their planets to seek help.

'But we can stop them,' said Jake. 'There is still time to resist. If we unite our colonies and combine our strength now, the Interstellar Navy will not dare to attack us. We must stand up to them and show that we are united, not by a government or a navy but by our independence.'

More leaders stood and clapped.

'I am here today to ask you to sign a treaty between our colonies, so we can send a message to Admiral Vantard and the United Worlds: if they attack one of us, they attack all of us. We stand together.'

A fierce applause broke out, which lasted for several minutes. Jake remained still, his head held high as the sound filled the grand chamber. His expression was strong and resolute, but inside his heart was doing cartwheels.

Chapter 23

The Altian Mechanic

Hector Rumpole took the microphone from Jake and the applause softened.

'Thank you, Jake Cutler,' said the mayor. 'These are grave times and your message is clear. We must act now to protect our colonies from the United Worlds and their naval warships.'

There were several nods in the crowd.

'Are you proposing that we create a fleet of ships from our planetary guard?' asked the chief of Ganton. 'If we do that, who will protect our colonies?'

'What about us?' exclaimed the premier of Travir. 'There are only two independent colonies in the second solar system. We're surrounded by United Worlds planets.'

'It's the same in the third solar system,' said the sheriff of Meltia.

Hector Rumpole held up his hands. 'My friends, I appreciate your concerns, but it will be far worse if we stand by and do nothing. It's a simple choice that we have to make today. Do we stand united, or do we fall divided? All those in favour of signing a treaty, raise your hands.'

Jake's eyes scanned the crowd. He spotted several hands shoot into the air without hesitation, followed by more as people made up their minds, until at least half of the room were in favour. Hector Rumpole raised his hand and Jake did the same. He knew that there would be some who were undecided.

'All those against?' asked Hector Rumpole.

Not a single hand lifted.

'In that case,' he said, 'we've just made history.'

There was a deafening cheer that shook the grand chamber. The prime minister of Santanova walked forward and grasped Jake's hand before taking the microphone from Hector Rumpole.

'What an incredible speech,' she said. 'Let this send a clear message to the United Worlds that we are here to stay. I have a treaty prepared, so we can put pressure on the Interstellar Navy to withdraw from Vantos. Jake, will you be the first to sign it?'

Jake stepped forward and accepted the document. He read it and signed his name at the end while the camera drones circled overhead. When he finished, he passed the treaty back to the prime minister of Santanova and returned to the small room, where

Kella and Nanoo were waiting. Jake closed the huge mahogany doors and howled with happiness. He had done it – he had convinced the leaders to unite against the Interstellar Navy. It was more than he had dared to hope for.

'That was incredible,' said Kella. 'You were magnifty.'

'Yes, how it feel to be famous leader?' asked Nanoo.

'I don't know,' said Jake, shaking with adrenalin. 'Kind of weird. It was strange enough being a wanted space pirate, but now everyone knows that I'm the ruler of –'

Jake checked the clock on the wall.

'What is it?' asked Kella.

'There's still time,' he said, stuffing his crown back inside his bag and rushing to the small black door.

Nanoo looked confused. 'Time for what?'

'To meet JD in the space docks.' Jake opened the door and paused. 'Are you coming?'

Were they doing the right thing by leaving the gathering before it had finished? Jake told himself that there would be plenty of time for handshakes and photos later. He had done his duty and united the independent colonies. Now he was doing something for himself. He just hoped that JD would be waiting for him when they reached the space docks.

The hover-car was still parked outside the Chamber of Parliament. Jake, Kella and Nanoo charged down the steps and wrenched open the back door. This time the crowd recognised Jake from the outdoor display screens. A group of reporters hurled questions, while their camera drones took pictures. Jake climbed into the back seat and instructed the driver.

'We need to get to Lugar Central Station fast.'

The hover-car raced across town and stopped outside the train station. Jake, Kella and Nanoo hurried to the platform, where the silver hover-train was waiting. Within minutes, they were hurtling back to the space docks.

'It nearly ten o'clock,' said Nanoo, as the Santanovan landscape smeared past the window.

'I know.' Jake glanced at his handheld computer and watched the seconds pass far too quickly.

Would they make it in time?

The hover-train arrived at the space docks and its doors slid open. Jake leapt on to the platform and sprinted into the main terminal, closely followed by Kella and Nanoo. The corridors were empty, as most people were in Lugar for the gathering. With seconds to spare, they arrived outside the main restaurant, fighting for breath and ready to collapse.

'We ... made ... it,' panted Jake.

'Is ... he ... there?' wheezed Kella.

Jake felt a rush of nerves at the thought of meeting JD. His curiosity burned as he peered through the restaurant door and located table six, but a house robot stood in the way, blocking his view. He caught sight of an arm, a human arm. There was definitely someone waiting for him.

'This is it,' he said. 'Wish me luck.'

'You want us go with you?' asked Nanoo.

'No,' said Jake. 'The message said to come alone.'

'Are you sure?' Kella looked concerned.

'Yes, positive.' Jake didn't want to scare off JD before they could speak. 'Listen, see if you can find a display screen with the *Interstellar News*. I want to know what the galaxy thinks of the treaty.'

Kella and Nanoo seemed reluctant to leave Jake, but they couldn't change his mind.

'We won't be long,' said Kella. 'Don't go anywhere without us.'

Once they had left, Jake swept back his thick brown hair and entered the restaurant. It was a wide room with large windows and round tables. Antique mirrors and paintings decorated the walls, while scented candlesticks sweetened the air. Apart from the person at table six, the restaurant was completely deserted.

Jake's heart nearly stopped when he realised that the house robot had moved out of the way. A man sat at the table with his back to the door. He was taking in the view of Santanova in the red morning light. His clothes were plain and grubby, but he sipped an expensive-looking cocktail. Jake marched across the restaurant to meet him.

'Are you JD?'

The man turned and smiled. It definitely wasn't the farmer John Daxton.

'Hello, my lord,' he said. 'It's been a long time.'

Jake recognised JD's heavily scarred face from the previous day, when he had looked surprised to see Jake in the space docks.

'Have we met before?'

'Please, take a seat.' JD waved to the house robot. 'Would you like a drink?'

'Apple juice, thanks.'

Jake found it strange to be served by a house robot after meeting the Hacker Jackers. He lowered himself into a chair next to the window, unable to take his eyes off JD. A few distant voices passed the restaurant door.

'My name is Jorge Dasch,' said the man. 'I don't expect you remember me.'

'Are you from Altus?' Jake was picking up hints of a clipped accent.

'Yes, but I've not been home for many years. I couldn't believe it when I heard our planet mentioned on the *Interstellar News* and then I spotted you in the space docks yesterday. I could tell that you were a Cutler. You look like your father, except for the hair and eyes of course.'

'Why did you leave Altus?'

Jorge swirled his cocktail. 'I was a mechanic aboard your father's ship.'

'You mean ...'

'That's right, I was there eleven years ago when the Interstellar Navy attacked.' Jorge pointed to the scars on his face. 'It's where I got these beauties.'

Jake steadied himself. It was as though he was meeting a ghost. Amicus Kent had not mentioned any other survivors, but how else would Jorge know about his father's ship?

'Why didn't you return to Altus?' asked Jake. 'You could have told everyone what really happened.'

'I ...' Jorge lowered his gaze. 'I couldn't.'

The house robot returned with a fresh apple juice. Jake thanked it and waited until it was gone before asking the question that was itching to escape his lips.

'Why not?'

Jorge shifted uncomfortably in his seat. 'I was afraid.'

'Afraid?' Jake was confused. 'Afraid of what? My uncle, Kear Cutler?'

Jorge nodded.

'Why would you be afraid of Kear unless you knew that he had sabotaged the ship?'

'All of Altus knew that Kear and Andras argued,' said Jorge. 'It was only a matter of time before someone tried to kill your father.'

'Someone? You mean Kear?'

'Yes, of course.'

There was something about Jorge Dasch that bothered Jake. The mechanic kept glancing out of the window, as though trying to avoid looking directly at him.

'Amicus suspected that my uncle had betrayed us,' said Jake. 'But what I can't figure out is how Kear could sabotage our shields and weapons when he was back on Altus. I mean, surely the crew would have checked the ship before launch, especially for such an important mission.'

Jorge's eyes widened. 'What are you saying?'

'The shields and weapons must have been disabled while the ship was in space,' said Jake, convinced that he was right. 'There must have been a traitor aboard –'

'I was a loyal servant of Altus.'

'You?' Jake stood up and drew his cutlass. 'Is that how you survived, when so many others died? Is that why you were too afraid to return to Altus? You were worried that my uncle would try to silence you, because it was you who left us defenceless.'

'Kear made me do it,' said Jorge, cowering in his chair. 'He told me that Andras and Amicus were preparing to sell out Altus. I thought that I was acting under orders from the Protectorate.'

Jake hesitated, the cutlass raised. 'What changed your mind?'

'I realised that it was a lie when Andras stood up to Admiral Nex, but it was too late. The Interstellar Navy attacked and I knew that Kear had used me.'

'My dad was a hero,' said Jake. 'He would have died before betraying Altus.'

'I know,' snivelled Jorge. 'I've had to live with the guilt for eleven years. I'm reminded of it every time I look in the mirror.'

Jake became aware of the house robot watching them, but it didn't matter. He kept a firm grip on his cutlass and prepared to strike the traitor. It seemed appropriate that he would do it with the sword of Altus.

'Because of you, Altus lost a great leader,' he said, his voice shaking with anger. 'Because of you, an Altian crew lost their lives. Because of you, I've lost my dad and I don't know where to find him.'

Jake took a sharp breath and swung the cutlass.

'He's not lost!' cried Jorge.

Jake froze in mid-strike, his blade inches from Jorge's head. 'What did you say?'

'He's not lost.' Tears coursed down Jorge's scarred cheeks. 'I've seen Andras Cutler since the attack.'

Jake had always believed that his father had survived. Had he finally met found someone who knew where to find him? It had to be a trick. How could he trust a traitor like Jorge Dasch?

'Liar.' Jake raised his sword.

'It's true,' said Jorge, talking fast. 'I knew your father. He often spent time with the crew. It was definitely him. His hair was longer and his nose looked busted, but it was him all right. I saw his head-cuffs.'

'His what?' Jake lowered the cutlass and eyed Jorge suspiciously. 'Was he some sort of prisoner? What happened to him? How did he survive?'

'I don't know.' Jorge fidgeted in his seat. 'He should have died in the asteroid field.'

'What about you? Amicus never mentioned another escape pod.'

'Amicus was halfway to Remota by the time I abandoned ship,' said Jorge. 'I've no idea where he landed, but I ended up in the desert. It was too dangerous to travel at night, so I stayed inside my escape pod until morning and then I dragged myself to the nearest farm. The farmer healed my wounds and dropped me at the space docks. I got work aboard a passenger ship and never returned.'

A team of planetary guards charged through the restaurant door. Jake knew it would be moments before they tried to take his sword.

'Where did you see my dad?'

Jorge spotted the planetary guards, but he kept talking. 'It was a few months ago, in a service port in the seventh solar system. He walked right past me with a friend. I guess he didn't recognise me with all of these scars.'

'What friend? Why was he wearing head-cuffs?'

It was too late. Jake was surrounded by four armed planetary guards, who were yelling at him to drop his weapon.

'OK, OK,' he said, throwing the sword of Altus on to the table and raising his hands.

If there was the slightest chance that he might see his father again, he had to stay alive. Jake's mind tried to process what Jorge had told him. Was Andras Cutler still in the seventh solar system? Had he been living near Remota the whole time? Who was the friend?

'Step away from the sword and put your hands behind your back,' ordered the nearest guard.

Jake started to panic. He couldn't afford to be arrested when he had service ports to search for his father.

'You don't understand,' he said. 'I'm the leader of an independent colony and I'm needed at the gathering.'

'Yeah, sure, whatever you say, my lord.' The planetary guard laughed. 'You're not going anywhere, sunshine.'

Jake backed away, but he was trapped by the window. Where were Kella and Nanoo?

'There's no need to arrest anyone,' said Jorge, rising to his feet. 'We were only having a minor disagreement, that's all, no harm was done.'

It was unclear if the guard believed this or not, because at that moment there was a blinding flash of light outside.

'What the gubbins is that?' exclaimed one of the guards, stepping away from the window.

A sound like thunder rumbled overhead and the whole restaurant shook. Jake shielded his eyes from the intense glare, which lasted for only a few seconds. He squinted through the glass to discover that the whole of Lugar was obscured by a giant dust cloud.

'No,' he cried. 'It can't be –'

There was only one thing that could have caused such a reaction, something that he thought he would never see with his own eyes. A mega-bomb had just destroyed Lugar. Jake watched the dust cloud climb into the sky and swell like a giant mushroom. A chorus of screams spread through the space docks, as people realised that the city was no longer there.

'It's gone … my family …' choked out one of the guards.

'What do we do?' asked another.

'We need to contact the duty officer,' said the nearest guard, backing away from the window. 'They will know what to do.'

The four of them rushed out of the restaurant, knocking over tables and chairs on their way. A siren wailed overhead and the lights dimmed to red, so the inside of the restaurant matched the sunshine outside. Jake stared in shock at the devastating scene, not wanting to believe that a million people had just lost their lives, including every independent colony leader in the seven solar systems. The mayor of Remota, the president of Reus, the prime minister of Santanova.

All of them, dead.

Chapter 24

Act of War

The cloud cleared to reveal a colossal crater where Lugar had stood moments before. Its charred surface was covered with debris, like a giant nest of rubble. Jake pressed his forehead on the glass. He was feeling weak and nauseous. What had he done? If it hadn't been for him, the leaders wouldn't have gathered there today. Come to think of it, if it hadn't been for Jorge Dasch, Jake would have died with them.

'You wanted me to leave the gathering early, didn't you?'

There was a loud click and Jake turned to find Jorge holding a laser pistol.

'I'm sorry, my lord,' said the mechanic, his voice now cold and detached. 'I needed you alive.'

Jake glared at him. 'Did you plant the mega-bomb?'

'No,' said Jorge. 'I was only instructed to keep you in the space docks until the Interstellar Navy arrives.'

'The Interstellar Navy?' Jake checked at the window. 'But they're not welcome here.'

Jorge smirked and the truth hit Jake like a laser bolt. All of the leaders were dead and the treaty was destroyed. The Interstellar Navy had not been waiting for the outcome of the gathering, it had been waiting until it was safe to attack Vantos. With the leaders out of the way, who would be able to stop the United Worlds from wiping out the independent colonies one at a time? It wasn't going to be a war, it was going to be a massacre.

'Thank you for listening to my confession,' said Jorge, keeping his laser pistol trained on Jake. 'It felt good to get that off my chest.'

'Drop dead, you wretchard.' Jake's shock had turned to anger.

Jorge tutted and checked his wrist computer. 'It shouldn't be long before the Interstellar Navy arrives. I contacted them the moment I saw you, though I had to pretend to be a fortune seeker from Yemet.'

'Why are you doing this?'

'Why?' Jorge had a wild look in his eyes. 'Because I'm sick of being a monster. I've suffered for what I did and now I want a better life. I'll use the reward money to pay for a new face and then I'll return to Altus. It should be safe now. If you're the new ruler, it means that Kear Cutler is either dead or in prison.'

'You don't have to look like a monster to be one,' said Jake.

'How dare you judge me,' snarled Jorge. 'You're the one hanging out with common pirates.'

'I would rather be a spacejacker than a traitor.'

Jake knew it was game over. He glanced out of the window and saw streams of ships evacuating the planet. At least Kella and Nanoo were safe in the space docks. But what about Callidus and Capio? Had they been in Lugar when the mega-bomb exploded?

'Admiral Vantard is looking forward to meeting you,' said Jorge, picking up his cocktail. 'I'm being paid an obscene amount of crystals to keep you here.'

'Blood money,' spat Jake with distaste. 'Why is everyone so obsessed with crystals?'

'If it makes you feel any better, they won't be worth as much on Altus,' sighed Jorge. 'How I've missed those crystal moons and that gold-dust desert.'

'You had better enjoy them while you can,' said Jake, through gritted teeth. 'Who knows how long I can resist maximum interrogation before I give away the location of Altus. Are you ready for the Interstellar

Navy to come bursting through the Tego Nebula, closely followed by the Galactic Trade Corporation?'

Jorge's expression faltered. He drained the rest of his cocktail and wiped his lips with his wrist.

'Perhaps it would be better to hand you over dead. I wouldn't get as much reward, but at least Altus would be safe.'

'You're too late,' said Jake, pointing at the window. 'A naval warship has just arrived.'

'What?' Jorge spun around, but there was nothing outside.

Jake seized the golden cutlass from the table and swung the blade. He caught the barrel of the laser pistol, knocking the weapon from Jorge's hand.

'Hey,' shouted the mechanic, as his pistol slid across the floor.

Jake lunged with his sword, but Jorge jumped clear and rolled over the next table. His scarred face scowled with a mixture of fear and anger. He picked up a chair and hurled it. Jake ducked and chased after him.

'That's two rulers of Altus you've failed to murder,' said Jake. 'You won't get another go.'

Jorge scattered tables in his attempt to escape, but trapped himself in the corner of the restaurant. He grabbed a tall iron candlestick and held it like a pitchfork. As Jake drew closer, Jorge jabbed the burning candles at him, spraying his face with hot wax.

'Let's see how you like a few scars,' sneered Jorge.

Jake cried out as the flames licked his cheeks and scorched his hair. He tried to fend off the attack, but his opponent was stronger than he looked. Jake retreated back and spotted a metal tray on a nearby table. He grabbed the makeshift shield and held it up as Jorge threw the candlestick like a flaming spear. Jake deflected the shot, but the force of it knocked him to the floor and on to his back.

Jorge sprinted back across the restaurant and recovered his laser pistol, which he held up triumphantly. He fired in Jake's direction, shattering an antique mirror and showering the floor with glass. Jake threw himself behind a pillar, cutting his hands and face on the broken fragments. He lay there, breathing hard, trying not to think about the pain.

'I should have known that you'd be hard to kill,' said Jorge. 'You're a survivor, like your father. But now I really must insist that you die, my lord.'

A few tables away, the candlesticks had set fire to a tablecloth and flames were starting to spread.

'Jake?' called out a voice from the doorway.

Kella and Nanoo had returned to the restaurant. Jake could make out their silhouettes through the smoke, framed by the light in the corridor.

'Watch out,' warned Jake. 'He's got a gun!'

Jorge fired at the door and one of the silhouettes fell backwards.

'No!' With a cry of rage, Jake climbed to his feet and charged at Jorge. He leapt off a chair and flew through the air, his cutlass held out in front of him.

Jorge turned at the last moment and fired a single laser bolt, hitting Jake in the stomach. A second later, Jake's blade sank into Jorge's chest and the pair of them crashed into the remains of table six.

'Jake?' cried Kella from the corridor. 'Are you OK?'

Angry flames flickered and crackled inside the restaurant as water rained down from the sprinklers. Jake lay on the floor with the sword in his hand, its golden blade coated in blood. Jorge Dasch was slumped next to him, dead. Jake looked at his stomach, where the laser bolt had struck him. There was a smoking hole in his uniform, under which something glistened in the light. It was his laserproof jacket.

'Wait there,' he shouted, coughing from the smoke. 'I'm coming.'

With a final glance at the traitor, Jake took the laser pistol and crawled towards the door. His whole body ached from cuts and bruises, but all he could think about was his friends in the corridor. If Kella was calling his name, then it must have been Nanoo who was shot.

'Is he alive?' asked Jake, reaching the entrance.

Nanoo sat against the corridor wall with his eyes shut. Kella crouched next to him, clutching her last crystal in her hand.

'I OK,' said Nanoo, holding his arm. 'Was that JD?'

'Yes, he was Jorge Dasch, a traitor from Altus. He reckoned that he had seen my dad in the seventh solar system a few months ago. I don't know what to believe.'

Jake noticed indigo blood seeping through Nanoo's lilac fingers.

'The laser bolt pierced his arm,' said Kella. 'I've slowed the bleeding, but we need to get him to a medical bay.'

Jake shook his head. 'We don't have time; the Interstellar Navy is on its way. If we don't get off this planet fast, we're all dead.'

'All right,' said Kella. 'But let's find a ship with some decent medical equipment.'

Jake and Kella helped Nanoo to his feet.

'Did you see explosion?' asked Nanoo, wincing with pain.

'Yes,' said Jake. 'Lugar has been destroyed. There's nothing left there now except a big grave.'

'All of those poor people,' said Kella. 'What are we going to do? Who will stop the United Worlds now?'

'I don't know.' Jake glanced back inside the restaurant. 'But we can't stay here.'

The three of them hurried along the corridor towards the docking terminals. Jake caught sight of the *Interstellar News* as they passed a display screen. It showed images of chaos and panic on the surface of Santanova, while a headline asked if the explosion was an accident or an act of war.

'How can you accidentally blow up a whole city,' shouted Jake at the display screen.

His eyes caught more words at the bottom of the screen: *Was Jake Cutler telling the truth? Is the teenage pirate really the ruler of Altus?*

'Ignore it,' urged Kella. 'We need to hurry.'

At the end of the corridor, they met a young planetary guard. Jake was about to ask for his help when the guard spotted the laser pistol and bloodied cutlass.

'Halt,' he ordered, raising his laser rifle. 'Drop your weapons.'

'It's OK,' said Jake. 'We're not your enemy.'

The guard held his position, his eyes fixed on Jake. He must have only been a few years older and probably had family in Lugar. In the background, there were shouts and screams as people flocked to the docking terminals. Nanoo looked pale and ready to collapse.

'Please let us pass,' said Kella. 'Our friend needs urgent medical aid.'

The guard glanced at Nanoo, who was dripping indigo blood on to the floor. He lowered his rifle and shook his head, as if doubting his own eyes.

'Who are you people?'

'It doesn't matter,' said Jake. 'All you need to know is that the Interstellar Navy is coming. You have to get everyone off this planet before it's too late.'

The guard hesitated for a second and then nodded. It might have been that he recognised Jake's face or uniform, or perhaps he was too distraught to argue. The guard rushed past and disappeared through a security door.

'Do you think he believed you?' asked Kella.

'I doubt it,' said Jake. 'Let's go, before he returns with friends.'

Jake and Kella carried Nanoo along two more corridors before they reached the docking terminals. As they entered, Jake's heart sank.

'We're too late,' said Kella.

Hordes of people were clamouring to board the last few vessels. Jake scanned the terminals, hoping to spot a gap in the crowd or a friendly pirate ship, but all that was left were a couple of passenger ships and a pleasure cruiser.

'That's it,' he cried, pointing at the end terminal. 'That's our way out, right there.'

'A pleasure cruiser?' said Kella. 'But it looks full and its doors are closed.'

'Hurry,' insisted Jake, letting go of Nanoo and sprinting towards the spacecraft. 'I know this ship. It's called the *Star Chaser* and it's from Reus.'

Jake had never been so pleased to see a spacecraft. He jumped up and down beneath the bridge window, waving his arms frantically. It had been months since he had last spoken with the crew in the space docks on Remota. He hoped they still recognised him with a burnt face. A small hatch popped open on the side of the hull and the co-pilot leant out, wearing a smart white uniform and matching peaked cap.

'Is that you, Jake?' he said. 'I saw you on the *Interstellar News*. What are you doing here?'

'I'll explain everything, but can you give us a ride?'

The co-pilot peered thoughtfully back inside the ship. 'We're already well over our passenger limit, but we should be able to squeeze three kids on to the bridge.'

Jake helped Kella to carry Nanoo to the side hatch, while the co-pilot extended a narrow ramp. The faces of frightened passengers were pressed up against the porthole windows and Jake knew that the ship would be packed inside. Where would they go? No independent colony would be safe from the Interstellar Navy now. All he knew was that they had to get away from Santanova.

As the three of them crossed the ramp, more people swarmed towards the *Star Chaser*, desperate to escape the planet. Jake had no idea what would happen to those who were left behind, but there was nothing he could do about it. If he stayed in their place, he would be captured by the Interstellar Navy and forced to reveal the location of Altus. Jake had hoped the other independent colonies would protect his planet. Now it was up to him to keep his people safe, whatever the cost.

The three of them entered the *Star Chaser* and the co-pilot sealed the hatch. It was bright and luxurious inside, with oak wall panels and brass fittings. Jake heard people banging on the hull outside, begging to come aboard, but their cries were drowned out as the pleasure cruiser pulled away from the terminal.

'If we take any more passengers, we won't make it to the next planet,' explained the co-pilot. 'Our supplies are already tight and there's only so much oxygen this ship can produce. Come on, let's get you to the bridge.'

'We need to use your medical bay,' said Kella. 'Our friend has a laser pistol wound.'

The co-pilot looked at Nanoo.

'Follow me,' he said, leading them through a crowded corridor of refugees. 'I'm guessing that your friend isn't from Santanova.'

'His name is Nanoo and he's a Novu alien from Taan-Centaur,' explained Jake.

The co-pilot swallowed his curiosity. 'Well, as long as he's not from a United Worlds planet.'

Kella went to say something, but Jake caught her eye and signalled for her to be quiet. If the crew found out that she was a United Worlds citizen, they might throw her off the ship.

Nanoo groaned in pain and stumbled. Jake caught him and Kella held a crystal to his wounded arm.

'Hang in there, Nanoo,' she said. 'Not far now.'

'Good,' mumbled Nanoo, his head flopping loosely on his shoulders, as though his neck had turned to rubber. 'I not feel well.'

'We'll catch the lift,' said the co-pilot. 'The medical bay is on the next floor.'

As the pleasure cruiser left the space docks, Jake listened out for laser cannon fire, but there was only the distant hum of the engine. He had half expected a fleet of naval warships to be waiting for them in space.

'Have you heard the latest?' said the co-pilot, once they were inside the lift. 'The Interstellar Navy has attacked Vantos.'

Chapter 25

Braving the Storm

Jake and Kella spent the next three hours in the medical bay, refusing to leave Nanoo's side. Kella had helped the ship's medic to clean and dress Nanoo's laser pistol wound before leaving him to rest. Nanoo was now snoring loudly on one of the recovery beds with a large chunk missing from his arm. Kella had also healed Jake's cuts and soothed his candle burns.

Jake watched over Nanoo while Kella rested on one of the empty beds. The lights were low and background music played gently through wall speakers. As he relaxed, Jake's mind filled with sickening images of the mega-bomb. A million people had been slaughtered by the Interstellar Navy and it was only the beginning. He wished that he had magical powers so he could disarm every naval warship with a click of his fingers.

In an attempt to distract himself, he opened his bag and pulled out his handheld computer. He wanted to see if Callidus had sent him an e-comm, so he would know if the fortune seeker was safe, but there was no stellar-net signal. Had the Interstellar Navy found a way to block it? Were Callidus and Capio OK? Jake stuffed the device back into his bag and took out his crown. He turned it around in his hands, watching the light reflect off its smooth golden surface.

It seemed appropriate that he should have a fake crown, because he felt like a phoney leader. What right did he have to declare himself as the ruler of Altus when he had abandoned his planet? A proper leader would have stayed and served his people, not run off with a crew of spacejackers. All of the real leaders had died at the gathering. If it hadn't been for Jake, they would still be alive now.

'Stupid thing,' he growled and threw the crown across the medical bay.

It clattered noisily in the corner of the room. Nanoo stirred and muttered something in his own language before going back to sleep. Kella grunted and rolled over to face the wall.

'How's it going?' asked the co-pilot, entering the room. 'Is your friend OK?'

'He's over the worst of it,' said Jake. 'But he's lost a serious amount of blood and we don't have any Novu plasma to replace it.'

'Where's his family?'

'His parents died in a shipwreck and the rest of his people live in another galaxy.' Jake looked at Nanoo. 'I promised to help him find a way home, but all I've done is get him shot.'

'I'm sure it wasn't your fault.'

'Of course it was my fault.' Jake struggled to contain his voice. 'I broke my promise, because I was too busy trying to find my father and unite the independent colonies. Nanoo came to Santanova and was hurt trying to help me. As for Kella, we were supposed to rescue her sister once we found Altus, but now she's locked up in Ur-Hal. I've not been a very good friend to either of them.'

'Garbish,' said Kella, sitting up. 'You and Nanoo are the best friends that I've ever had. If it hadn't been for you, Nanoo would be dead and I would be a slave, so stop feeling sorry for yourself and work out how to fix things.'

'Fix things?' blurted Jake. 'You might not have noticed, but all of the independent colony leaders are dead.'

'Not all of them,' she said pointedly.

'Me?' he said. 'What can I do? I have no idea how to contact the other colonies. And even if I did, why would they listen to a thirteen-year-old spacejacker from Altus?'

Kella folded her arms. 'You convinced the leaders at the gathering.'

'Yes, but that was different,' he said. 'Hector Rumpole was there to back me up.'

The co-pilot had heard enough. 'Jake, I've tried to ignore the fact that you brought weapons and a wounded alien aboard this ship, but what's this about slavery and spacejackers? What happened to the nice kid who used to hang out in the space docks on Remota? We had better go and see the captain.'

Jake knew that he had said too much, but it was too late to take any of it back. He straightened his uniform and went with the co-pilot, leaving Kella to look after Nanoo. It would have only been a matter of time before the crew discovered the truth anyway. Jake hoped the captain would give him a chance to explain. He followed the co-pilot along the corridor and up three more floors to the top deck. The *Star Chaser* was far cleaner than the *Dark Horse*, but not nearly as cosy. It smelt of cleaning fluid and Jake was worried about leaving handprints on the oak wall panels.

The bridge itself was bright and spacious, with a curved ceiling and a panoramic window. It boasted the latest technology, including holographic displays, asteroid sensors and a long-range scanner that would have made Farid sick with envy. There were at least eight shipmates in smart white uniforms operating the various equipment. Jake doubted that it had a multi-barrelled laser cannon hidden behind a secret panel.

A tall, thin man with a trimmed grey beard stood in the centre of the room. His uniform was decorated with gold buttons, braids and tassels, as well as the emblem of Reus: a yellow circle on a blue shield, representing the planet's famous sunshine and clear skies. Jake guessed that this was the captain of the pleasure cruiser.

'Jake Cutler?' he asked, as they entered. 'Ruler of Altus?'

'Yes, that's right.'

'My name is Captain Dan Swan. I'll assume by the colour of your eyes that you're also the teenage space pirate that we've been hearing so much about on the *Interstellar News*.'

Jake stood proud. 'Is that a problem?'

'I've got more important things to worry about than spacejackers,' said the captain. 'We've received reports that Santanova has been surrounded by naval warships. It looks as though we got out just in time.'

'Is everyone OK?' asked Jake.

'No shots have been fired, but the Interstellar Navy is demanding that the planetary guard hand you over, or face the consequences. Would you mind telling me why those wretchards want you so badly?'

'It's not me they're after,' said Jake. 'They want my planet and its three crystal moons.'

'Are you telling me that Altus really exists?'

Jake nodded.

'And you're its rightful ruler?'

Jake nodded.

'As well as a space pirate?'

Jake nodded.

All of the shipmates on the bridge stopped what they were doing and stared at him.

'But you're just a kid,' said the co-pilot.

Jake shrugged. 'That doesn't stop it being true.'

'Or change what has happened,' said Kella, appearing in the doorway with Nanoo.

'And it not bother Interstellar Navy that Jake is a kid,' pointed out Nanoo, who still looked pale as he held on to the hatch frame. 'He still tortured if they catch him.'

The captain regarded the three of them. 'When I was your age, I was playing games on the stellar-net.

Not running around the galaxy trying to unite the independent colonies.'

'Will you help us?' asked Jake.

'Help you?' said Captain Swan. 'To do what? Naval vessels are gathering around our home planets. It looks as though the Interstellar Navy will take out the independent colonies one solar system at a time, starting with the seventh. My wife and two daughters are on Reus, but what can a pleasure cruiser do against a fleet of naval warships?'

'What about the other colonies?' asked Jake.

'I'm sure they would help us,' said the captain. 'If we had a way to contact them. But I expect that most of the colonies are busy appointing new leaders and protecting themselves. Who would they follow into battle? All of the leaders are dead.'

'Not all of them.'

Jake looked out of the window at the convoy of refugee ships and knew that he had to do something, otherwise the Interstellar Navy would sweep through the galaxy like a space storm, leaving behind a trail of death and destruction.

'You?' said the co-pilot.

'Who else is there?'

Kella and Nanoo joined him in the centre of the room.

'What you saying?' asked Nanoo.

'I'm going to make this right,' said Jake. 'I don't care what it takes, I'm going to fix things.'

Kella placed a hand on his shoulder. 'You can count on us.'

'No,' said Jake. 'Not this time, shipmates. Nanoo, we'll drop you off at Shan-Ti monastery, where you can wait for your people. Kella, we'll find the *Dark Horse*, so the crew can help you to free your sister, Jeyne.'

Nanoo frowned. 'Don't be a guffoon.'

'Yeah,' said Kella. 'Do you really think we'd turn our backs on you now, when you need us the most?'

'This isn't a game,' insisted Jake.

'We know,' said Nanoo. 'And we not playing.'

'We're in this together, you astronut.' Kella wore a stubborn expression as she planted her hands on her hips.

Jake should have known that his friends would never abandon him. It was a good job, because if he was going to fly into the heart of the storm, he would need all the help he could get.

'In that case,' he said, turning to face Captain Swan, 'I suggest that we drop the passengers off at on Shan-Ti.'

'What about the rest of us?' asked the captain.

'We're going to contact the independent colonies,' said Jake. 'And then we're going to war.'

Captain Swan considered this for a moment. 'Aye, my lord.'

Jake retreated to the rear wall with Kella and Nanoo, while the crew set course for Shan-Ti.

'Are you sure you're ready for this?' asked Kella. 'It's one thing to rule a planet, but another to lead every independent colonist in the galaxy.'

'I have to be ready,' said Jake. 'We need to stop the Interstellar Navy and I'm the only one who can do it.'

'You might not be leader,' whispered Nanoo.

'What do you mean?' asked Jake.

'If your father alive, then he rightful ruler of Altus, not you.'

'Nanoo's right,' said Kella. 'You're more of a pirate prince than a king.'

'It doesn't matter,' said Jake. 'The independent colonists need a leader now, so until we find my dad, they will have to make do with me. It's about time a descendant of Zerost made a stand.'

The whole thing seemed so incredible, but at the same time, it felt as though it was meant to be. It was no longer about warning people; it was about fighting for what was right. Jake had learnt that from the cyber-monks on Remota, when they died to protect him. He would stand up to the Interstellar Navy on behalf of those who had been murdered by them, as well as the millions more who were still in danger.

It was hard to imagine a galaxy without independent colonies, where the Interstellar Government ruled every planet. If that happened, there would be nowhere for Jake and the others to hide from the Interstellar Navy. Any hope of finding his father and leading a normal life would be lost forever. And then how long would it be before the Galactic Trade Corporation discovered Altus and mined its crystal moons to the core? If Jake wanted to protect his friends, his father and his home planet, he would have to save the entire galaxy, starting with the seventh solar system.

No more running. No more hiding.

'The Interstellar Navy is going to be sorry that it ever messed with a space pirate,' he said out loud.

Jake would find a way to contact the independent colonies and stop the Interstellar Navy. The seven solar systems weren't perfect, but they were worth fighting for. Whatever happened in the days to come, he knew that Kella and Nanoo would stand by him. They would risk their lives and brave the storm together.

As friends.

As shipmates.

As spacejackers.

HAVE YOU READ JAKE'S FIRST ADVENTURE?

OUT NOW!